DANNY ORLIS
AND
EXCITEMENT AT THE CIRCLE-R

DANNY ORLIS

AND

EXCITEMENT AT THE CIRCLE-R

BERNARD PALMER

Danny Orlis and Excitement At The Circle-R
© 2024 by Bernard Palmer
All rights reserved. First edition 1971.
Second edition 2024.

Cover image: Adobe Firefly
Character illustrations: John Ball
Editor: Charlene Miskimen

Aneko Press Youth

www.anekopress.com

Aneko Press, Life Sentence Publishing, and our logos are trademarks of Life Sentence Publishing, Inc.
203 E. Birch Street
P.O. Box 652
Abbotsford, WI 54405

JUVENILE FICTION / Religious / Christian / Action & Adventure

Paperback ISBN: 979-8-88936-064-3
eBook ISBN: 979-8-88936-065-0
10   9   8   7   6   5   4   3   2   1
Available where books are sold

CONTENTS

CHAPTER 1

A LETTER FROM THE ROPER RANCH

It was time for evening devotions at the Danny Orlis home. The family had finished dinner and Danny had the Bible in front of him, but he did not begin to read immediately. He was thinking about something else.

"I got a letter from your Uncle Clarence Roper in Texas today," he told the Davis triplets.

"You did?" DeeDee exclaimed, leaning forward excitedly.

"How're Maria and Philip and Aunt Carmen?" Doug wanted to know.

"Yeah, we haven't heard from them since they went back to Texas last month," Del added.

"I guess the kids both got a big kick out of Blackie and being up on the Angle. They said it was the best summer they'd ever had."

"It was an exciting summer," Del agreed. "I can say that much."

Kay, who had been listening to the conversation without taking part in it, turned to Danny. "That isn't what you wanted to tell the kids, is it?"

"Not exactly."

They eyed Danny with growing exasperation. There were times when he would tease them that way, hinting at something but never coming right out and telling them until they were so excited they could hardly stand it.

"Do they want us to come down and visit them again?" Del wanted to know.

"During school?" DeeDee countered. "We couldn't go now, even if they asked us."

"Well, they didn't ask you," Danny continued. "So you don't have that to worry about."

Doug groaned. "I thought maybe we'd get to go back to the ranch again. We haven't been there for a long time."

"What *did* Uncle Clarence write about?" DeeDee insisted.

The smile faded from Danny's face. "I really shouldn't have teased you this way. It's really a prayer request, but it has excited me more than any letter that I've gotten in a long while." He took the envelope from his pocket and pulled out the long, handwritten letter. "You know, there's been a big change at the Circle-R Ranch since your Uncle Clarence became a Christian."

The triplets nodded.

Their uncle had always been a fine fellow even before he became a Christian, but he got mad after their cousin Phillip and Aunt Carmen confessed their sin and gave their hearts to Christ and he was real hard on them. He didn't want them to go to church or listen to a radio preacher, and above everything else, he hadn't wanted Del and Doug and DeeDee around. He blamed them for what had happened.

But they knew that things were different around the Roper ranch now that Clarence had become a Christian too. Phillip had told them all about it when they were up at the Angle a few weeks ago. Now that his sister, Maria, was a Christian too, that would make things even better.

"Your Uncle Clarence wrote all about the trip he and your Aunt Carmen took to Guatemala last summer. He said that visiting the field where your folks lost their lives shook him more than anything else. He said his first thought was that he should sell the ranch, go to Bible school somewhere, and go back to Guatemala to take up the work that your mother and dad left."

"Is that what they're going to do?" Del asked.

"Is that the prayer request?"

"I think he decided God wasn't calling them in quite that way. He's got some ideas for helping the missionaries in Guatemala in a financial way, but he seems to be the most concerned about the people who live in the area around the Circle-R. He feels that God would have him work right at home. And he's asking us to pray for him – for the whole family as they witness to their neighbors."

"That *is* exciting!" Kay broke in. "I don't suppose there's ever been a strong Christian witness in that area where the ranches are so large and the people live so far apart."

"He wants us to pray for the Flores family. I guess they live right on the ranch."

"That's Mack Flores," Del said. "You remember who he is, Danny? His mother is cook for the ranch hands."

"They were the ones we found living under that old bridge, Danny," DeeDee explained. "Mack's father had died and the family was heading north to try and find a relative who would help take care of them. Their old car broke down and they couldn't go any farther."

"Mack is the one who was stealing food for his mother and his brothers and sisters, wasn't he?" Kay said.

Doug scooted his chair closer to Danny's. "Wouldn't that be great if Mack would become a Christian, too? I'm going to pray for him every night."

"So am I," Del and DeeDee both agreed.

"And we want to pray for Mrs. Flores and the rest of the kids too. They need Christ as badly as Mack does."

"That's exactly right, DeeDee," Kay observed. "I think it would be nice if we would all agree to pray for them every single night, don't you?"

CHAPTER 2

A NEW VENTURE

Twelve-year-old Mack Flores eyed the Circle-R ranch house uneasily. He didn't know for sure if he liked all the changes that had come about since Mr. and Mrs. Roper came back from their trip.

They had been good to him and his mother and the younger kids since they came to the ranch to live. He didn't have any complaint about that. Mr. Roper had given them a nice house to live in and paid his mother enough for cooking for the cowhands so she could buy all the food and clothes they needed. She even had some money hidden away in the bottom of an old jar in the kitchen. Mack wasn't supposed to know about that, so he pretended it wasn't there. They had more of everything than they needed. No one had ever treated them half as well as the Ropers did.

But that didn't keep Mack from being disturbed. Since Clarence Roper and his wife got back from their vacation, the ranch owner had been talking to him about sin and Jesus Christ and going to heaven. Mack didn't understand everything Mr. Roper said, but he understood enough to make him feel as though he was one of the worst guys in Texas. Some nights he couldn't sleep or anything.

He started to talk to Phil Roper about it one day but he soon stopped that. Phil was as bad as his father when it came to that religious stuff.

Mack turned away from the house and made his way down to the barn where his younger brother, Eduardo, was getting grain for the horses. He didn't have to worry about Eduardo preaching at him. He was as shook up by Mr. Roper's preaching at him as Mack was.

"About done, Eduardo?" His young voice rang through the big barn.

"I could use some help."

"That's why I came out here. Is Phil or Mr. Roper around?"

Eduardo came into view at the corner of the manger. Sweat glistened on his dark forehead.

"Are *you* ducking them too?"

Mack saw what his brother was doing and set to work, methodically measuring oats for the grain boxes.

"Not exactly. I just don't want to talk to them tonight."

"I think I'll tell them where you are," Eduardo

retorted, laughing. "That would be a good joke, wouldn't it?"

Mack snorted. He didn't want to see Mr. Roper right then, but he didn't like the idea of Eduardo making fun of the ranch owner, either. He had been too good to them.

"Phillip came in looking for you a little while ago. I thought you'd gone somewhere."

The older boy stopped what he was doing. "What did Phil want with me?"

"He just wanted to talk to you, I guess. He told me that they're planning a surprise in a week or two."

Mack's eyes gleamed. "What kind of a surprise?"

"That's all he'd tell me. He said that I'd have to wait until they were ready to let people know about it."

Mack thought about that. He couldn't figure out what sort of a surprise the Ropers could have, and he especially couldn't figure out why they would want to keep anything a secret on the ranch. They'd never done that before. If it was somebody's birthday it might be a little different, but it wasn't.

"Was it a surprise for you or me, Eduardo?" he asked.

"Why should it be for you?"

"He came out here looking for me, didn't he?"

The younger boy frowned. "I guess he did, at that."

At the supper table that night Mack could think of little else. He had already decided that the surprise had to be for him. Why else would Phil come out to the barn looking for him?

Maybe Clarence Roper was getting some new saddle horses and was going to give him one to take care of and ride. He'd talked about that a few times lately. Or maybe the rancher had decided to have him start riding the range with the men. Mack had talked with him several times about letting him quit school and go to work as a cowhand. He could herd cattle as well as any man. And he'd be able to rope too when he got a little bigger.

His mother wouldn't like it if he didn't go to school anymore, but he was tired of studying. And why would he need more education than what he had already? He had decided a long time ago that he was going to be a cowhand for Mr. Roper when he got old enough.

Come to think of it, Mack reasoned, he had overheard the foreman tell Mr. Roper that he was shorthanded. The rancher must have been thinking about it and decided to let him go on the payroll. Why else would Phillip come looking for him?

* * *

However, Clarence Roper and his family had been talking about something entirely different the night before, and that conversation had been the basis for Phillip's remark to Eduardo.

"I've tried to talk with Mack and the rest of the Flores family," Clarence said, his manner betraying his concern. "But they act as though they don't even understand what I'm trying to tell them."

"I've talked to Mack a couple of times myself," Phil added. "But I didn't get anywhere with him either. He acted like he had to get away from me fast."

"I didn't listen at first when Mother and Phil and then you started talking to me, Daddy," Maria put in. "It must be as hard for them now as it was for me before I became a Christian. I didn't understand for sure what it was all about, and I was afraid to let Jesus have control of my life. I kept telling myself that I wanted to run it my own way."

"I felt the same way," her mother said.

"I'm sure we all did," Mr. Roper went on. "That's a favorite trick of Satan's. But now we've got to try and figure out how to make them see that accepting Christ as their Savior and living a Christian life is the only way they can be truly happy."

"What about that Sunday school you've been talking about, Dad? Do you think it would help the Flores family?"

"It might help them and a lot of the rest of our neighbors, if we could get them to come. The way I see it, starting a Sunday school here is about the best way we've got to reach them."

Carmen was not so sure that Mack and his brothers and sisters would come. "I've talked to Mrs.

Flores. She's a very nice lady, but she's antagonistic toward the gospel. She keeps saying that they have their own religion."

"You could tell them that they *have* to come, couldn't you, Dad?" Maria asked.

Clarence straightened in his chair and tugged at his earlobe. "I suppose I could. But I'm not sure that would be wise."

"Why not?"

"God doesn't force us to become Christians, and I think we ought to use that as our example in dealing with others. I don't think we should force Mack and his brothers and sisters to come to our Sunday school, as much as we'd like to have them there."

"But we can try to talk them into coming, can't we?"

"We sure can. And we can pray that God will make them *want* to come."

Listening to the children and her husband talk made Carmen so happy she could scarcely contain herself. Imagine Clarence being interested in leading a Mexican family – or anyone else, for that matter – to Christ. It scarcely seemed possible that he was more concerned than anyone else in the family. Briefly she wondered if this wasn't a dream that would be over with the ringing of the alarm in a few minutes.

But it wasn't. She was awake and the entire family was gathered about the table discussing the organization of a Sunday school on the Circle-R.

"There are a lot of kids around here who might

like to have a Sunday school to go to," Phil continued. "That new hand you hired has got a kid about Maria's age. She'd probably come."

"And it wouldn't be too far for the Harrises to ride over from the Lazy-H," Maria said. "And some of the other ranch kids could be invited. I don't know why we didn't think of this before. It's going to be a lot of fun."

"It is, at that," Clarence told her seriously, "but we've got to remember, Maria, we're not organizing this Sunday school just to have a good time. We've got to do it as a means of presenting Christ to those who don't know Him."

It was difficult for Phil and Maria Roper to keep from telling the Flores kids about the Sunday school, but they had decided to wait until Saturday to let them know. Clarence thought it would be better not to give them too much time to think about it before the time came to go.

They didn't have much opportunity to talk to anyone else about it either until that same Saturday. That morning Phil and Maria were up an hour earlier than usual. They got their chores out of the way and rode over to the Lazy-H to talk to the Harris kids about coming to Sunday school the next day. They were so excited the ride seemed endless.

"And after we go there," Maria said, "we can ride to the house where their foreman lives. He's got a boy about your age."

"That's right," her brother replied. "I'd forgotten about him." He considered the matter thoughtfully. "I think some of the other men who work for Mr. Harris have kids too. You know, we might be able to get five or six for Sunday school from the Harris place alone."

"Wouldn't that be wonderful?"

"And that's just one ranch," Phil said. "Why, we ought to get quite a crowd after a while. I'd like to fill our living room with people tomorrow morning. Wouldn't you?"

"Dad would sure be happy."

They left the lane and rode up the dusty gravel road in the direction of the neighboring ranch. A funnel of dirt swirled across the road ahead of them, leaped over the ditch, and waltzed away among the mesquite and sage brush.

"What do you think they'll say when we ask them about coming over to the Circle-R for Sunday school tomorrow morning?" Maria asked thoughtfully.

Phil's fingers tightened on the saddle horn. "They always have come over for anything we've ever invited them to. I'm sure they'll be there. We probably don't have any better friends anywhere than the Harrises."

"I know, but this is different."

"They might be glad for a chance to come over and learn about God."

"I hope so. I've been so excited about going calling today that I was hardly able to sleep last night."

"Me too." Phil slouched in the saddle, thinking. "You know, Maria, after we've had our Sunday school going for a while maybe we can get a little church organized."

"Do you suppose we could?" Her eyes danced.

"It wouldn't take very many if everybody helped. We could build it on our ranch, maybe, and build a house for the preacher and everything."

"And maybe we could get a minister with a girl about my age so I would have a Christian girl for a friend."

"Or maybe we could get someone with a *boy* about your age." Phil's grin was broad and teasing. "And you could have a Christian boyfriend. How does that grab you?"

She stuck out her tongue at him.

"Or would you rather have Bob Harris?"

"Is that supposed to be funny or something?"

They rode on for several minutes without speaking. By this time they were going up the lane to the Lazy-H ranch buildings. Bob and Sally, the Harris kids, were in the yard and came running over to them.

"Hi."

"I'm so glad you came," Sally exclaimed. "I've been so lonely for company, Maria. It's been ages since anyone has been over to see us."

Phil swung out of the saddle as though he planned to stay a while, but Maria did not dismount.

"I'm sorry, but we can only stay a minute this

morning," she said. "We just came over to invite you to our house tomorrow."

"Sounds like a good idea," Bob replied quickly. "What's going on? You havin' a ranch rodeo or a barbecue?"

Maria was about to answer him, but the words caught in her throat and her cheeks were flaming. She didn't know why that would be. There wasn't anything to be embarrassed about. They were just inviting their friends to something that was going on at the Circle-R.

"We've decided to start a Sunday school at the Circle-R beginning tomorrow," Phil said. "And we'd like to have you both come over in the morning, and your Mom and Dad too, if they'd like to."

"*Sunday school?*" Bob wrinkled his nose distastefully.

"You mean Sunday school – like in a church?" Sally broke in.

"Well," Maria said uneasily, "I guess you could say that it's going to be sort of like church, only it isn't."

"What do you mean by that?"

She cringed involuntarily. She had not expected them to question it, as though they didn't like the idea of coming over to the Circle-R for that purpose.

"We'll sing songs and study the Bible," Phil added.

"That doesn't sound like much fun to me."

"Oh, but it is. You'll both enjoy it." He turned to his sister for support. "Won't they, Maria?"

She tangled her small fingers in her horse's mane nervously, and for a moment she wished that she hadn't come.

"I think you would like it," she murmured reluctantly.

"You will come, won't you?"

Bob did not say for sure that they wouldn't come, but he didn't agree to be there either.

"I don't know exactly what we're going to be doing around here tomorrow. Dad may decide to go someplace else or have company or something."

Phil could not hide the disappointment in his eyes. Bob hadn't even asked when the meeting would start. That showed he didn't really plan on coming.

"It'll be starting about 10:30," he continued, "if you do decide to come."

Sally Harris seemed a little more interested than her brother. "It sounds as though it might be fun."

Phil and Maria stayed at the Harris ranch for a few minutes before going on. Sally and Bob wanted to know what they had been doing and how they liked school and if anyone interesting had been over to visit them lately. It wasn't long until they excused themselves and rode down to the foreman's house to talk with Eddie Norton.

Eddie was in Phil's grade at school and they knew each other well. He was even more friendly than Bob and Sally had been, but it was obvious that he wasn't any more interested in coming over to the Circle-R for Sunday school than they were.

"I doubt if I can make it, Phil. Sorry."

"It's not all that far."

"I know, but that's the only day that I don't have to go to school or work. I like to sleep until noon and then get up and do something I really want to do."

Phil tried to press him, but it was impossible to get a commitment from him. It seemed as though he was being nice to them only because they were neighbors.

On the way to the next ranch Maria turned to Phil. "Eddie didn't sound very interested in coming, did he?"

He did not answer immediately.

"Do you think he'll come?" she asked hopefully.

"I wish he would, but I sure don't expect him." Phil's face clouded. "To tell you the truth, I'm beginning to wonder if anybody else will be there except our own family."

Maria fought against the ball of ice in her stomach. "Mack and his family will be there," she said optimistically. "At least we'll have them."

"I'm not so sure about that. I talked with Mack again this morning, but he acted just like the others. I wouldn't be surprised at all if they stayed home too."

His sister's face wrinkled curiously. "I wonder why God doesn't make *everybody* want to come to Sunday school."

Phil laughed. "It would sure make our job a lot easier if He did."

CHAPTER 3

A SLOW START

That Sunday morning was an exciting time on the Circle-R Ranch. A tense expectancy gripped the Roper family. They got up as early as usual and had everything ready for Sunday school by 10:30.

Phil and Maria had gone through the only songbook in the house and had picked out several of the more familiar songs, and their mother had made copies of the words for everybody.

"I wish we had a guitar or an accordion or something to help with the singing," Maria said. "I think it sounds so much better when there's an instrument."

Phil laughed. "What good would that do? None of us can play!"

Their dad looked up. "I think I could play any of them better than I'll be able to teach a Sunday school lesson."

"You'll do fine," Carmen assured him.

He had been reading and rereading the portion of Scripture he planned to use for the Sunday school lesson, but not without a certain amount of protest. He tried to get Carmen to agree that she would take over for him, but she flatly refused to do so.

"No, Clarence," she told him firmly, "it's your place to lead. You're the man of the house. It's your responsibility to take care of it."

"I can ask somebody else to do it if I want to." He spoke defensively.

"Besides, it was your idea to have a Sunday school."

"I thought you would help me when I suggested it. I thought we all were in this thing together."

"We are," Carmen continued. "And if some children come, I'll teach them. I've worked up a lesson for them, myself."

Desperation gleamed in his steel gray eyes. What she said about helping with the children was true. He had seen her studying something the last few days. And if some of the younger parents came, there should be someone to take care of their kids, someone who could teach them a simple Bible verse and talk with them about Jesus.

"Maybe *I* ought to teach the kids," he muttered, "and let you teach their parents."

"I'd like to see that." She laughed at him tolerantly.

Clarence glanced at his watch and went back to studying again. A few minutes later he closed his Bible and went to the front room to look up the long lane that ran across the prairie to the graveled road beyond the first row of hills.

"It's almost 10:30," he said aloud. "I thought somebody would be here by this time."

"So did I," his wife said. In spite of herself, some of her uneasiness showed through. Clarence and the kids had been so excited about the Sunday school and getting it organized that they had been unable to talk about anything else for the past couple of weeks. But she knew their neighbors. They had never shown any interest in spiritual things. She had tried to talk with a few of the women about her own decision to give Christ her life, and they had scarcely been courteous to her. She heard afterward how they laughed at her behind her back. That hadn't mattered particularly to her then and it didn't bother her now, but she was concerned as to whether they would come to the Sunday school.

It was going to be awfully difficult for Clarence and the kids if nobody showed up. They had put so much work into it and had been so confident of success. She had been praying for the last week that there would be a good turnout.

In spite of her own hesitancy in talking with their neighbors about the Sunday school, Maria had absorbed her Dad's enthusiasm. She had no doubt whatever but that they would have a tremendous crowd from the very first Sunday and it would build from there. Phil, however, was much more pessimistic, even more so than his mother.

"I don't know whether we're going to have anyone come today or not," he said for the third or fourth time. "We sure didn't get much encouragement from the ones we saw. Nobody acted excited about it."

Maria spoke hopefully. "But they all said that *maybe* they would come over, and I'm sure that some of them meant it."

He shrugged. "I hope you're right about it, but I don't know whether we're going to have anyone or not."

"We'll have somebody here," Clarence put in confidently. "We've been asking God to send them over. We've got to believe that they'll come."

At 10:30 there was a knock at the door and Clarence went to open it.

"Well, it sounds as though we're going to have somebody here besides ourselves," he murmured.

A wide grin split Maria's pretty face. "Oh, I'm *so* glad."

Clarence Roper opened the door. "Hello, Mack. I'm glad to see you. Come on in."

The Mexican boy sidled uneasily into the room. As he did so he glanced from one person to the other, dark eyes solemn. He looked as if he wanted to turn and run.

"You're just in time," Phil said, going over to him. "We're about to start."

"I thought maybe I'd come for Sunday school," he explained as though they were wondering why he had come at that particular time.

"Fine. We're sure glad to have you." Clarence Roper's big voice boomed. "That's real good, Mack. But how about your mother and the rest of the kids? Are they coming too?"

Mack shook his head.

"No, I don't think so. Mama thinks they better not come." He paused, uncertain as to whether he should continue or not. Then he went on doggedly. "She says she doesn't want me to come either, but she won't tell me that I have to stay home since I am the man of the house."

Clarence frowned. He had thought there might be some opposition from some people, but he hadn't expected any from Mrs. Flores. He thought she was so grateful for the fact that he had given her a job on the ranch that she would be sure to be there with all of her children. He rather expected Mack to furnish more opposition than his mother.

"So I came," the boy added.

"That's great. We're glad you did."

They went into the living room and sat down.

"Did I get the time wrong?" Mack asked in his Spanish accent. "Did I come too early?"

"Oh, no." Clarence seemed as happy at having him there as he would have been had the entire room been filled with their neighbors and friends. He got a chair for himself and set it across the room from the others, so he faced them.

"Do you think anyone else will come?" Maria wanted to know.

Clarence glanced at his watch. "It's after 10:30. I think we'd better start. If they come in late, they'll just have to miss out on part of the Sunday school. That'll make them want to get here on time next Sunday."

He turned to his wife.

"I'm afraid I'm going to have to have a little help with the singing. You know I can't sing."

She stood up and said, "I'll lead the singing this week and Maria or Phil can lead next week, OK?"

When the hymns were finished Clarence Roper led in prayer and taught the Sunday school lesson, using the picturesque, expressive language of the range.

"When a maverick wanders away, the cowhand has to go after him, even if it means that he has to leave the rest of the herd and ride off into the mesquite to find him."

Phil and Mack both nodded that they understood. Neither of them had done much cattle herding, but they knew from listening to the men talk at night what had to be done to take care of their herds.

"That's what Jesus Christ does with us," Clarence continued. "We've wandered away from the life we ought to live. And we've gotten down into sin. We have tried to go it alone just like the headstrong little calf that doesn't know anything. And all we do is get ourselves lost and in such a mess that we can never get back to the rest of God's herd on our own. We'd die out in the mesquite of sin if Jesus didn't shake out His loop and come riding out to rope us and bring us back to His herd where we belong."

Phil had listened to a lot of messages on the radio and had gone to church whenever they were in a place where they could, but he had never heard the Bible explained in quite the way that his dad was explaining it that morning. Even Mack, who had come so uneasily, listened with great interest as the ranch owner continued. Soon the hour was over and Clarence asked for a closing song and a short prayer to end the first Sunday school meeting. As soon as it was over, Mack got to his feet quickly and started for the door, anxious to get out of there; but Mr. Roper followed him. He put his big hand on the Mexican boy's shoulder with real affection.

"I want you to know that we really are glad that you came this morning, Mack," he said. "I don't know what happened to the others we invited. They probably had something come up at the last minute."

"I wouldn't be too sure," Phil mumbled.

But his dad ignored his remark. "I'm going to be looking for you to come back next Sunday."

Mack nodded gravely. "Maybe I'll come again. I like to hear what you say."

"You don't know how good that makes me feel."

"Yeah, we're glad you came," Phil added. "And be sure and bring Eduardo and your mother and the rest of the family the next time."

The boy flashed a weak smile and disappeared on the run. For a few moments Phil and Clarence stared after him.

When they turned back, Clarence saw that Maria was almost in tears.

"And now what's the matter with *you*, young lady? Didn't you like the way I handled our new Sunday school?"

"It's not that." She had to fight to be able to continue talking. "I thought it was wonderful."

"Then show a little of it on that pretty young face of yours." He tilted her chin upward and dried her eyes with his handkerchief. "This is no way to show me how much you enjoyed our first Sunday school meeting."

She stared at him helplessly. "But Daddy–" She choked and had to start once more. "But Daddy, there isn't any use for us to keep trying. It's like Phil said. Nobody is going to come over here to Sunday school. They just aren't interested. We're wasting our time and–and making ourselves a laughingstock by trying."

Clarence did not share their discouragement, however. In fact, he was smiling pleasantly. "Now wait a minute, Maria, before you decide that we'd better quit. God has never promised us an easy time of it when we try to serve Him."

"I know, but I thought that at least there would be one family who would want to come to our services."

"We had Mack. That was a start. And he listened carefully. I was watching him."

"He just came because you've been so good to him and his family. That's all."

"We don't know that; but even if it's true, it doesn't make any difference. He heard the gospel." Clarence took her into the living room where they sat down. "This is something new, Maria. We can't expect people to come flocking to it the first time we ask them."

"I suppose you're right." She agreed with him verbally but was still unconvinced. "But, Daddy, nobody came today. We didn't have anyone here except Mack. I'm so disappointed I could cry."

"It isn't anything to cry about. We ought to praise God that Mack came to our Sunday school. You've got to remember that his mother didn't want him to, but he came anyway. We have that to be thankful for."

"You really can't count him."

"Why not? He isn't a Christian and he came. I don't see how you can say that we can't count him. He's almost at the top of my prayer list."

"I know, but I think Mack came because he likes us all so much. It wasn't because he really and truly wanted to."

"Then we ought to be thankful that he likes us so much," her dad said.

"I'm sorry." She wiped away the tears and tried to smile.

"I remember how I used to be not so long ago, honey. I did everything I could to show that I didn't want to have anything to do with Jesus Christ. If your mother and Phil had given up on me, I probably wouldn't be a Christian now." His big smile made them all feel better. "No, if the people don't come, as much as we'd like to have them come, it just means that we're going to have to work a lot harder on them, that's all. We've got to keep after them until they decide that they want to come."

Maria's fleeting smile returned; and Carmen, who had been listening to her husband and daughter, broke in. "And right now we can help speed things along by asking God to make our friends want to come."

Maria's smile widened as she gave her mother a hug. "I see now that you're right." There was a long pause. "Having Sunday school here on the ranch really makes Sunday seem like a very special day, doesn't it?"

CHAPTER 4

A JOKE BACKFIRES

During the next few weeks, the Roper family continued to visit the neighboring ranchers, urging the people to come to Sunday school. When Phil and Maria went to school, they gave all of the kids special invitations.

"You mean you're really serious about that Sunday school?" Bob Harris demanded incredulously. "You're *still* trying to get people to come to it?"

"Sure," Phil retorted. "And if you'd come a few times you'd find out why. You'd like it as much as we do."

Bob snorted. "Not me. I don't want everyone saying I'm a fanatic."

The color sneaked up Phil's neck and spread across his cheeks. "Who's a fanatic?"

"That's what people are saying about you. They say your whole family has gone nuts on religion."

Phil thought about that. His dad had said that there would be those who talked about them. Phil honestly hadn't believed that it would happen or that he would be as upset about it if it did. But it did bother him. It bothered him so much that at that moment he almost wished they had never started the Sunday school. If he had kept the kids from knowing that he was a Christian, they wouldn't be able to make fun of him the way Bob Harris was doing. He supposed all the other guys who knew him felt the same way about him.

"You're not going to get *me* over to your Sunday school. I can tell you that much."

The Sunday school was still limping along, with scarcely any more attending than had come to the first meeting. On some occasions there was another one or two who came out of curiosity or to try to gain favor with Clarence Roper. Some of the new ranch hands tried that, but they soon quit when they found that it didn't get them any raises or help them to get easier or more interesting job assignments.

Mack attended most of the time, although he continued to skip out as soon as the meeting was over and would never talk to any of them about what went on there or what was said in class. The Ropers figured that his mother didn't get much information out of him about the Sunday school either. Once in a while she asked Carmen what they did at Sunday school.

"Why don't you come and find out?"

Mrs. Flores was flustered by the invitation. "Oh, no, I couldn't do that. My church wouldn't like it. I mean I have so much to do that I don't have time for such–such doings as Sunday school."

Carmen tried to answer her objections, speaking to her in Spanish; but it seemed as though Mrs. Flores had determined not to listen or understand. She always sat stiffly, her gaze riveted on the distant wall, until her employer's wife finished talking about God. Then, stiffly, she would rise to her feet.

"I must go now, Senora. Adios."

Carmen Roper felt a heaviness in her heart as the woman left and went back to the little house where she lived with her children. It was so difficult when there was no response.

Phil thought his dad ought to urge his men to attend the services.

"They'd sure get something out of it," he said, "even if they just came because they knew you wanted them to."

But Clarence did not want to do that. He invited the cowhands. In fact he went further than that. He saw to it that each one, individually, knew that he was welcome. But that was as far as he would go. He didn't insist that they be there, nor did he grant any favors to those who did come.

"If they come to our Sunday school," he said, "I want them to come on their own. It wouldn't do any good to get them there against their wills because

I'm the boss and they think they have to attend if they want to hold down their jobs."

Phil Roper finally voiced the question that had been plaguing him and the rest of the family for a long while. "Are you sure that this isn't a waste of time, Dad? Do you think there's any use in keeping on with the Sunday school?"

"Keep on with it?" Clarence echoed. "Do you think we ought to quit?" His tone indicated that he had never considered the matter of quitting.

"Are we doing any good?" his son persisted. "Do you believe we'll *ever* get anyone to come?"

Clarence's smile came and went. "I don't know for sure whether we can get them to come or not," he said quietly. "And I'm not particularly concerned about what we can do or can't do. I know that God can get them here. We've got to trust Him and depend on Him to help us. That's the only way we can make our Sunday school touch people's hearts. If we have to depend on our own strength, we're whipped before we start."

"I know all of that, but we've gone everywhere asking people to attend and we've gotten nobody. They start laughing at us now when they see us coming." He pulled in a deep breath. "I don't think there's anyone in the whole valley besides us who cares whether there's a Sunday school on the Circle-R or not."

Clarence Roper's lips tightened. It was a moment

or more before he spoke. If he was discouraged, he didn't show it, at least for no longer than an instant.

"There's one thing a rancher has to learn, Phil," he said, "and to learn well. He's got to have courage to stay in there and fight and never give up."

Something about Clarence's courage and determination bothered the boy. "But this isn't like working cattle," he protested. "A guy can figure out what a cow or a bunch of steers is going to do. But with people it's different. Sometimes I think some of them refuse to come just because we want them to come so bad."

Clarence was still not disheartened. "We'll just have to pray and work a little harder, that's all."

* * *

The following Saturday, Clarence Roper had Phil and Maria do some work around the ranch instead of riding out to invite their friends and neighbors to Sunday school.

"I thought you said that we shouldn't give up, Dad," Phil exclaimed.

"Who said anything about giving up?" His grin was wide and friendly. "I just decided that we'd do things a little differently this time. I decided to have you stick around here and I'd go out and do the inviting for this Sunday."

"You'll probably find out that it isn't as easy as it seems," Phil muttered.

"Now you are encouraging. Why don't you show a little optimism?"

"I just don't think you'll have any better luck than we did, that's why."

Clarence grew serious. "You will pray for me, won't you?"

"Sure we will, Dad."

Carmen and Maria added their promises to pray for him to Phil's promise. As Mr. Roper pulled out of the yard, Carmen turned to Maria and Phil.

"I'm glad Dad is going to do the inviting this time, aren't you? I think it's always good to change when you run into problems."

"They'll come for Dad," Maria said confidently. "He'll be able to say the right things to make them decide to come."

But Phil was still far from convinced. "I hope you're right, but I don't think they're going to come because Dad invites them any more than they did when we asked them. The whole trouble is that nobody's interested in Sunday school, that's all."

The three of them watched until the pickup jounced out of sight across the hills. Carmen feared that she was echoing Phil's concern inwardly. It seemed so hopeless to try Sunday after Sunday to get anyone to come to the services. Clarence's confidence was still unflagging, but she was afraid that after a while he too would be discouraged. He was so anxious to see the Sunday school grow. It would be a terrible thing if nobody came that Sunday either.

"You know," she said quietly, "I think we ought to go in now and ask God to help Dad get some of our neighbors to come to our Sunday school tomorrow, don't you?"

They nodded solemnly. After all, they had promised him that they would pray for him. They had to keep that promise.

When the three of them finished praying, they felt better. It wasn't as though they had firm confidence that there would be a big crowd at the next day's service. Nothing like that. But they had done what they could to help, and they had the feeling that somehow God was going to work. They didn't know how just yet, but they felt that He was going to give them results for their efforts.

It was almost dark when Clarence returned to the Circle-R that evening. He came striding into the house, whistling happily.

Maria jumped to her feet and ran to the kitchen as soon as she heard him. "Hi, Dad!" she cried.

"Hi, yourself!" He picked her up and held her in his arms momentarily. She was a tall, slender twelve-year-old, but he still picked her up and hugged her on occasion, just as he did her mother. And she was glad he did. He was just about the best dad in all the world.

"How many promised to come to Sunday school

tomorrow?" she wanted to know. "How many said they would be there?"

"How many do you suppose?"

"Three," she said hesitantly. "Four, maybe."

"You sure don't have much confidence in me."

Excitement gleamed in her eyes. "Were there more than that?"

"I'm asking you how many you think I got to agree to come."

"I don't know. Tell us, Dad! Tell us!"

When he saw how excited she was, he was sorry for having misled her. "You'll have to forgive me, Maria. I was just teasing you. I really didn't have much in the way of results."

"How many promised to come?" she insisted.

"To tell you the truth, there were only one or two families who seemed interested and I'm not at all sure whether they'll come or not."

Tears appeared in the girl's eyes. "I don't know what's the matter with them. Don't they know that it's for their own good?"

"We can't blame them for not wanting to come, honey. It's only natural that people resist the gospel. But they'll be coming one of these days. Don't you worry about that."

"What makes you so sure?"

"Because we've all been praying they would come," he said simply, "and I know that God will answer our prayers."

Clarence Roper's confidence buoyed up the spirits of everyone. That night they had a brief time of prayer asking God to work in the hearts of the people he had visited that day.

The following morning a few minutes before time for Sunday school, a car from the Harris ranch pulled into the yard.

Maria squealed with delight when she saw it. "Look, Dad!" she cried. "They did come, after all! The whole Harris family is here!"

Clarence Roper went out to greet them. In spite of the fact that he had been confident God was going to work, his own spirits soared.

A lanky, sandy-haired rancher slid out from under the wheel.

"We decided to come over and see what's going on," Mr. Harris said. "Your family's been so excited about this Sunday school that you've come over practically every week to invite us. We want to find out what it's all about."

"We're sure glad to have you. Come on in, Sam. We'll be starting in a few minutes."

Sam Harris hesitated. "Anybody else here?" he wanted to know.

"You'll be the first, but there may be some others along any time."

"They're supposed to be–" He caught himself quickly. "I–I mean, there's – I figured there would be some others coming this morning."

If Clarence Roper noticed what his neighbor said, he paid no attention to it. He urged the Harris family to go into the house and make themselves at home.

They did as he suggested, lining up on the sofa in front of the picture window. Sam looked at his watch uneasily.

"What time do you start, Clarence? Is it to be 10:30 or 11:00?"

"We always start at 10:30," Clarence explained. "We figured that would give people a chance to get home in time for dinner."

Sam grinned impishly. "You mean you're not inviting us to dinner? Doesn't a meal go with your preaching?"

"We'd be delighted to have you stay with us for dinner," Carmen said quickly.

"Sam!" His wife was indignant. "I've never heard of anything so rude."

"We can't let a good chance like this go to waste. I figure it's worth a meal to come over and let Clarence preach at us."

"You might have a point at that." Clarence Roper didn't seem to mind that his neighbor was doing everything he could to make fun of him. "It's 10:30 and a little after. I think we'd better start."

Sam looked about. "You mean this is *all* that's going to be here?"

"Unless they come in late."

As usual, Clarence was the Sunday school

superintendent and teacher. Sam Harris leaned back in his chair with obvious amusement as Clarence called the little group to attention for an opening prayer. A wide grin twisted Sam's weathered face and once or twice he made remarks under his breath. No one could hear exactly what he said except his wife. Her cheeks were scarlet and her eyes angry.

"Sam!" she whispered. "If you don't stop that, I'm going to leave!"

For a moment he was silent, but his grin left no doubt as to what he thought of the Sunday school meeting. Phil read the look with considerable uneasiness.

If there had been any other ranchers in attendance at the Sunday school that morning, the Roper boy would have been certain they had come because of some scheme they had concocted to pull a joke on his dad; but that couldn't be the reason. Sam Harris was the only one there. A joke wouldn't be any fun unless everyone was around to laugh.

But, come to think of it, Sam did act as though he expected someone else. He looked out the window every once in a while and glanced at his watch.

Clarence had Carmen lead them in several songs before he took over. Then he began the program with a little story that brought out a special point in the Sunday school lesson to follow. Then he took up the offering.

"Things must be rough for you on the ranch, Clarence," Sam said. "If you've got to stoop to this to get money. You must have to take up three or four offerings a morning, don't you? You're sure not going to get enough to do any good out of this bunch."

Clarence only grinned.

"Have you tried to see the bank? They might loan you a little money if things are going so tough for you."

"They've never gone better," Clarence said mildly. "The Lord has blessed us in a wonderful way. And, for your information, we're going to use this money to reach the people around here for Christ."

After the offering Clarence launched into the Sunday school lesson. At first Sam Harris continually made wisecracks under his breath. Everything Clarence said was subject to his scorn, as though ridicule could blunt the things the tall, broad-shouldered Christian was saying.

As Clarence continued, Sam grew more sober and quiet. By the time the hour was over he was considerably subdued. Everyone else was visiting, but Sam called Clarence into the kitchen.

"I've got to tell you how sorry I am, Clarence. I didn't know it was going to be anything like this."

Mr. Roper stared at his neighbor. "What do you want to apologize to me for?" He couldn't think of what Sam had done to him that would warrant an apology.

"I'd rather take a beating than to tell you this, but I didn't bring the family here this morning because I wanted to attend your Sunday school."

"It doesn't make any difference why you came. We're glad to see you and hope you'll be back."

"You may not want us back when you find out why I drove over this morning. After you left the Lazy-H yesterday, I decided this was a good chance to pull a joke on you; so I went over to visit Tom and Edgar myself. I talked them into promising to come over here to see me break up your Sunday school today. Now I'm glad they didn't show up!"

Clarence could scarcely believe him. His eyes widened and he sucked in his breath sharply. "That's hard to believe, Sam."

"It's true just the same. That's the reason I came here this morning. It's the *only* reason I came."

"Well, I'm glad you were here anyway, and I hope you'll come back."

Sam Harris found his gaze and held it momentarily. "You mean that's all you're going to say?"

"Why? Should I say something more?"

"Aren't you going to blow up about it?" he asked.

"What good would that do?"

Sam shook his head. "Now I *do* believe that you're different than you used to be, Clarence. I've always told people that this religion of yours would last only until you got mad enough to blow up. And I figured that this would be enough to do it."

Clarence Roper put an arm on his friend's shoulder. "Only God could tame that hideous temper of mine, Sam. I can tell you that right now, if you didn't know it already."

"I didn't think anything could tame your temper, Clarence. But now you've shown me that I've been wrong. Something has changed you."

"Not something," Clarence Roper corrected. "Someone. And that Someone is Jesus Christ. He gave me a new life."

Sam pulled in a long breath and expelled the air in a thin stream.

"We'll come back all right." The rancher spoke quickly. "Only we won't be coming back to cause you a bad time. From what I've heard and seen this morning, you've got something here that won't hurt any of us."

Clarence Roper beamed. This would be something to tell Carmen and the kids, he decided. It would be a good lesson to make them see how important it is to stick to a thing. He might even be able to use it in opening exercises sometime if Sam didn't mind. He decided that he would ask his friend about it after he and his family had established the habit of attending the Circle-R Sunday school regularly.

CHAPTER 5

MACK IS MISERABLE

After Sam Harris brought his family to the Circle-R for Sunday school that day, they came almost every Sunday. Bob Harris got their foreman's son, Eddie Norton, to come and once in a while Eddie's dad and mom came too. It wasn't long until other families from the neighboring ranches started coming.

Maria was more excited and happier about it than anyone else in the Roper family.

"Isn't it marvelous, Dad? People we didn't dream of are coming. And the kids don't tease us about it anymore, either."

"It sure is great." He dropped to an easy chair and put his feet up on a stool. "It's really a lesson in faith and answered prayer, isn't it?"

She sat down in a chair across from him. She didn't know exactly what he meant, but she supposed he was talking about the fact that she had gotten so discouraged when no one came at first.

"I was beginning to get concerned about our Sunday school too, Maria," her dad told her. "But God heard our prayers and answered in a way we would never have thought of."

"Yes, and I'm so thrilled about it. Maybe we'll have some Christian neighbors before long."

"Now that would be something to be happy about."

They continued to pray regularly for the Sunday school and the people who would be coming. Once some of the neighbors got started coming, they drove over almost every Sunday morning for the service. Once in a while, when the weather was nice, Clarence and Carmen would have a barbecue or a picnic for everyone after Sunday school. It gave the people a chance to get together and visit as well as an opportunity to hear about Jesus Christ.

The fact that families from other ranches started coming had an effect on the men who worked on the Circle-R. They too began to attend the Sunday school. Most of them didn't come regularly, but there were always some of them present.

Mack didn't come regularly at first. He would be there for a Sunday or two and then would miss a couple of times. He too acted as though he was afraid to come. He would linger nervously outside until the music started. Then he would slip in and sit in the first empty seat he came to, holding his battered hat in a skinny brown fist. His gaze was usually fixed on the floor, and there was no indication that he was even hearing what was being said.

Everyone else took part in the singing, but not Mack. He sat rigid, his mouth clamped shut; and as soon as Sunday school was over he scooted out before anyone could talk to him. In spite of that, however, he soon began to attend with regularity.

In the beginning Mack was the only member of the Flores family who would come to Sunday school, but after a time Eduardo and some of the younger kids began to come. They did so timidly at first, sitting at the back, as close to the door as possible. And every once in a while they would leave before Sunday school was over.

Mrs. Flores was the last person on the ranch to start coming. When she did, it was with such hesitance that Carmen and Clarence were afraid she would only make it once. She acted as though she was doing something she shouldn't be doing and would be afraid to come again.

The rest of the Flores family was just as shy as Mack. Eduardo, who was the next younger to Mack, wouldn't even come into the house for Sunday school for a while. He would stand outside the door listening to the singing. He would listen to the Sunday school lesson too, as long as the Ropers didn't let on that they knew what he was doing. If that happened, he would flush nervously and move silently away.

It took a great deal of effort to get him to come to Sunday school at all.

But after two or three months the Flores kids began to look forward to going to Sunday school. Phil Roper didn't think it was because they were interested in hearing about Jesus Christ, although they seemed to enjoy some of the Bible stories. It was just that Sunday school was something for them to do, something to break the monotony of life on the ranch, a chance to meet some of the kids from the other ranches.

Phil was more concerned about Mack Flores than any of the others, for some reason. His thoughts were always on his Mexican friend. And at family devotions he asked the others to pray for Mack.

"I know he's interested in the gospel. I can tell that by the way he acts. But for some reason he seems to be afraid."

"It's because of his background, Phil," Clarence said. "The way I understand it, the family comes from a pagan village in Mexico. He's been taught to be afraid of other gods."

"We all ought to pray for him, shouldn't we, Dad?" Maria asked.

"Of course we should. It's an excellent idea. But I don't think we have to wait until we get together to pray for him. We ought to pray for him personally too – each one of us."

"I have been praying for him every day," Phil

continued, "but it doesn't seem to do any good. He's just as far away from confessing his sin and taking Christ as his Savior as he's ever been."

"That doesn't mean that *nothing* is happening in his life," Carmen broke in. "He could be fighting against the gospel right now. Maybe that's the reason he acts the way he does."

Phil frowned. "I hadn't thought of that."

"That was the way you were, wasn't it, Dad?" Maria asked. "And it was the way I was too. You don't know how terrible I felt when we would have devotions and I was the only one at the table who wasn't a Christian. I used to think that I couldn't stand it any longer, that I had to get up and run as far as I could so I wouldn't have to listen to the Bible reading and prayer."

"That's right," Clarence said. "The fact that we haven't seen any change in Mack doesn't mean that God isn't working or that nothing is going to happen in his life. Why don't we pray for him right now?"

They bowed their heads and Phil led them, asking God to continue to work in Mack's life, to soften the boy's heart and bring him to the place where he was willing to confess his sin and put his trust in the Lord Jesus Christ to save him. Usually only one prayed for a specific request, but this particular night they were all so concerned for Mack that they each prayed for him.

After that they prayed for Mack every night at

family devotions and also for the rest of the Flores family. Maria assured her brother that she too was praying for Mack and his family every night.

"And sometimes when I think of it during the day I ask God to work in Mack's life right away," she said.

"Thanks." His warm grin said more than his voice.

He too prayed for Mack every night. He not only asked God to work in the Mexican boy's heart, but also that He would give him a chance to talk to Mack about Christ. In bed it was fairly easy to plan what he would say to Mack and how he would manage the conversation. It was different when he and his friend were together.

Several times he tried to maneuver the subject in a way that would give him a chance to talk with Mack about his need of Jesus, but for some reason he wasn't successful. He didn't know whether Mack saw what he was planning and avoided it or if it only seemed that way. But there was no opportunity to talk with Mack about his spiritual need. In spite of himself, Phil grew increasingly discouraged. Serving God certainly wasn't as easy as he thought it would be. He couldn't understand it.

* * *

It was Sunday morning and Mack Flores was waiting outside the Roper house for Sunday school to begin. The wind whipped in from the west picking up bits of sand and dirt as it roared over the parched prairies. Mack hunkered in the shelter of the house, away from the wind.

It was a bad day. He didn't suppose there would be many people coming for Sunday school that morning. He knew he wouldn't be going if he had very far to travel. It sure didn't make sense for people to come as far as some of them came just to go to Sunday school.

Now if they were coming for a rodeo, that would be different, or a barbecue or coyote hunt. There would be some sense to traveling a ways for something worthwhile like that. But Sunday school? He couldn't figure it out.

For that matter he couldn't figure out why he kept going, Sunday after Sunday. It wasn't because he enjoyed it so much, that was sure.

He didn't know why he felt so strange about the meetings, either. He liked Clarence and Carmen Roper, and Phil was probably the best friend he had, in spite of the fact that Phil was quite a bit older than he was. He thought maybe he went because he liked the singing. That was one thing he missed about their village back in Mexico, the times when they would get together and sing.

He didn't know the words to the songs they sang in Sunday school, let alone what they meant, but the tunes were catchy and every once in a while he would find himself humming one of those songs the Ropers sang.

But there was something else that made him uneasy about going there. Sometimes after he heard the lesson he felt so bad over some of the things he had done and what his life was like that he could not even sleep. When that happened, he decided that he wasn't going to go back to that Sunday school anymore. He didn't care if the Ropers did have it or if they were his best friends.

Once or twice on a Sunday night his mother heard him tossing restlessly and came to the bedroom door. He guessed that she thought he was sick or something.

"Mack?" she called out nervously. "Mack?"

He opened one eye speculatively and tried to act as though he had been asleep. But, down in his heart he knew that he hadn't fooled her. She had heard him turning and twisting in bed and knew that he was awake.

"What is it, Mamma?"

"Can I come in?"

"Sure, but I'm all right."

She opened the door and stepped into his room so the rest of the kids would not be awakened by their voices. "Something is wrong, Mack," she said. "No?"

"Not with me." The lie burned his lips. But he could not tell her that he had been awake. If he did, she would have to know why he wasn't sleeping.

Ever since Papa had died she was so nervous about things like sickness.

"You were not up a little while ago?" she persisted. "You didn't get out of bed just now?"

"Nope." He was glad for the darkness to hide the flush of his cheeks. He was glad too that he could answer her question truthfully. At least he was not adding another lie to the sin of his life. "Why would I be out of bed, Mamma? It is still dark."

Still his mother did not move. "I hear somebody get out of bed, I think. Maybe it was Eduardo."

"What would he be doing up in the middle of the night, Mamma?"

"I hear something," she persisted.

"Well, it wasn't me, that's for sure." He lied again to her. Was there no end to saying things that weren't true? Would he never stop doing bad things?

She started to leave but turned back.

"If there is something wrong, Mack," she asked, "you will call me, no?"

"Sure, Mamma. I'll call you, but there's nothing wrong. Maybe you heard the wind rattling the windows or one of the dogs outside the house."

"It was no wind I hear," she murmured, "and no dog."

"I'll call you if there's anything wrong."

After she was gone, it was all that he could do to keep from crying out and telling her the truth and asking her forgiveness. But she would not understand how he felt. She kept talking about their own reli-gion. After they left Sunday school she would tell them that it was all right to go, but they should not think about following the way the Ropers followed.

If he told her he was sorry for lying to her, she would have to know everything. She would make him tell her how going to Sunday school made him feel and how this new uneasiness and longing in his heart troubled him. And if he let her know those things, she would feel so bad she would cry.

He didn't think she would scold him. She hadn't done that since his papa died. But it would make her feel bad, and he couldn't bear to do that. She had had enough things hurt her the past few years without him doing anything to add to her problems.

There was one thing he had already decided. He wasn't going to that Sunday school anymore. He couldn't stand feeling the way he did. Right after breakfast the next Sunday morning he was going to slip away and he wouldn't come back until he was sure the meeting was over. He wasn't going to have Clarence Roper and the others get him so upset again that he wasn't able to sleep.

All week he went over in his mind what he was going to tell Phil if he asked him about being there Sunday morning, but when the rancher's son did ask him, he couldn't refuse.

"I – I don't know for sure," he stammered.

"You'd better be there. Dad's got something special

planned, and he'd feel terrible if you weren't there. That's for sure."

"I may have some work to do or something."

"You know how he feels about working on Sunday. The only things he wants done around the place on Sunday are things that have to be done, like feeding the cattle."

Mack stared at the ground and mumbled, "If I don't have to work, I guess I'll be there."

"You won't have to work. I'll guarantee it."

That settled that, Mack realized. He would have to be at Sunday school whether he wanted to or not. There just wasn't any way that he could dodge it, whether he wanted to go or not.

He didn't know why he couldn't be like Eduardo. If he didn't want to go any place, he just didn't go. And he didn't care whether anyone liked what he did or not. But Mack couldn't do that.

And now the time for the Sunday morning service had arrived and he would have to go and sit through another Bible lesson again. He didn't think he could stand it.

If he hadn't told Phil that he would sit with him, he could have turned and fled the way Eduardo would have done. He just might do that anyway, he reasoned. There was no rule that said he had to go to Sunday school every Sunday, and especially when it shook him up the way it did.

He had almost convinced himself that he should

leave when the barn door opened and a familiar figure stepped out into the sunlight. It was Phil Roper.

"Hi, Mack. I've been looking all over for you."

The color inched up Mack's neck and into his cheeks as he returned Phil's greeting.

"I was just going up to the house."

"Fine. I'll go with you." He fell in beside the slight, handsome, young Mexican, matching him stride for stride. "Dad was just telling me that some new people are supposed to be coming to Sunday school this morning. I guess they moved into the old Meyers place a couple of weeks ago."

Mack scowled. Phil sounded as though he thought Mack was as religious as he and his dad. Why would he be telling a thing like that? It didn't make any difference to him one way or the other. He didn't care whether anyone else came or not. Now that he thought about it, he figured it would be better if there was only a small crowd. If people would quit coming, Clarence Roper might get discouraged and quit having Sunday school.

Reluctantly Mack went in with his older friend and sat down. He wanted to take his usual place near the door so he could get out fast when the meeting was over, but Phil had another idea. He insisted on going right down to the front. They were so far from the door he wouldn't have a chance of getting out of there, even if he wanted to. He would have to stay right there and endure it.

Mack fidgeted uneasily.

Clarence Roper led in prayer and again asked Carmen to lead the singing of a few hymns. He was doing a little better in that department himself, but he still didn't feel that he dared get up in front and try to lead.

"Now," he said when the last hymn was finished, "we'll all stand and read the first sixteen verses of the fourteenth chapter of John."

Mack was glad that he didn't have a Bible. At least he wouldn't have to read those verses out loud. That was one good thing. But it was not to be that way. As everyone stood, Phil leaned over to him.

"Here," he whispered, "You can borrow my New Testament if you want to."

Mack tried to shake his head in refusal, but Phil wasn't paying any attention to him. He thrust the Testament into his hands.

"Let not your heart be troubled," they began to read, "ye believe in God, believe also in me."

As they read Mack fell silent. He wondered what that meant. It sounded as though God was going to take care of whomever He was talking to. He said something about going away to build mansions for them, and when He got done He was going to come back after them.

Mack knew what it was like not to have a place to live. He and Mamma and the kids had been in a fix like that when they got as far as the Circle-R ranch on their way north from Mexico and their car broke down. He remembered how desperately frightened he had been.

It would be wonderful to have one of those places that God was preparing. And if God loved him so much that He would fix him a house all his own, He would love him enough to see that he had something to eat and plenty of clothes to wear. It would be nice not to worry about things like that anymore.

Mack breathed deeply. He wondered if Mamma knew about heaven. They had a good place to live, it was true. But it didn't belong to her; and if she left the Circle-R or quit working there, she wouldn't have a place to live anymore. So this place that God was fixing must be a lot better than the house they had now.

Mack thought about that momentarily. He couldn't help wondering who would get the houses God was making. It would probably be people like Clarence Roper and his family, he decided. They were good people. God would want to do nice things for them.

But what about him? The thought stabbed through him. Was he going to get one? Would God fix a place for him to live when he lied and did so many bad things?

He didn't dare think about it.

CHAPTER 6

AN UNWELCOME GIFT

The small group of people in the Roper living room finished reading the Bible portion and sat down. The ranch owner asked his wife to lead them in another hymn, and then he began to teach the Sunday school lesson.

Everyone listened intently, except Mack Flores. He squirmed miserably in his chair and looked about, suddenly frantic. He couldn't stand it any longer. He had to get out of there!

He didn't know why, but in that instant he hated Clarence Roper. He supposed he really hated the things Mr. Roper was saying. But whatever the reason, he couldn't stand him anymore. He couldn't sit on the front row and look up into that smiling face. He couldn't listen to the ranch owner's calmly confident voice. He *had* to get out of there! He couldn't stand another minute of it!

It was all right for Mr. Roper to talk the way he did about dying. He knew where he was going. He didn't have anything to worry about. But if what he read in the Bible was true, Mack knew where he was going too. That was what bothered him so much.

The Ropers had reason to get excited about those houses in heaven that Jesus said He was fixing. They would get one for sure. Maybe they would each get one.

But not him.

God wouldn't have a place for him there. He wouldn't want Mack to be in one of the houses that He was preparing for the people who loved Him. The boy knew that he wouldn't even dare ask if there was one for him. He was too wicked for God to give anything.

His lower lip quivered; and, for a moment, he turned to stare at the tall boy beside him. Phil didn't seem to be concerned at all. Mack wished, desperately, that he could be that way too.

But he couldn't.

He felt that he had to get up immediately and leave, but how could he? He was sitting on the front row. If he left now he would cause a terrible commotion and have to answer all kinds of questions afterward. Everybody would think he was sick or something, especially his mother. She worried about things like that.

No, he would have to stay. He didn't have any

choice except to stick it out and try to keep from listening to what Mr. Roper said.

He thought he could do that. He had managed it before, when someone was lecturing him about something.

At first that worked quite satisfactorily for Mack. Doggedly he kept his mind on the things he was going to do as soon as the meeting was over. He would go saddle up one of the horses while his mother was fixing dinner. And when he had eaten, he would go off on a long ride alone. He'd get so far from the ranch that nobody could find him to talk to him about anything.

But, as Clarence continued talking, his words began to filter through Mack's consciousness.

"Jesus tells us that He *wants* us to be with Him in heaven," he was saying, "but that doesn't necessarily mean that we *are* going to be there. We are sinners and God cannot be in the company of sin."

Mack swallowed hard. That ended any chance he would have of getting to heaven. He knew that he was a sinner.

"But God didn't stop there. If He had, it would be too bad for all of us. He knew we could never be good enough to go to heaven, so He sent His Son, the Lord Jesus Christ, to live on earth and die for our sin and be raised to life again. If we confess that we are sinners and put our trust in Jesus to be saved, God will save us. We can become a child of His and go to heaven. One of the mansions He is preparing for His children will belong to us."

In spite of his determination not to hear anything that Mr. Roper was saying, he was clinging to every word. He didn't understand it all. Actually, he guessed that he understood less than anyone else in the room. He couldn't understand how God could send His Son to die on a cross, for one thing. It didn't sound right that God would do that.

Yet his heart was touched in a strange way. He really wanted to be like the Ropers. He wanted to be able to *know,* right then, that he was going to heaven. It would be wonderful not to have to be afraid of dying.

Still there were all the bad things that he had done, like stealing things to eat when his mother and the little ones didn't have any food and lying to her. There were other things too, so many of them that it hurt even to think about them. God wouldn't want to save him. It made his heart ache.

Mack read that portion of Scripture again, carefully, pronouncing each word to himself. As he did so the words drove even deeper into his heart. He was reading it a third time when the service was over.

Phil saw what he was doing and mentioned it. "Would you like to keep my New Testament for a while?" he asked quietly.

Mack flushed. He didn't think that Phil or anyone else knew he was reading the Bible. He had become so interested in it that he wasn't aware that anyone else was in the room. He looked up quickly to see if his mother was watching. But, she had turned and was making her way toward the door. He was glad for that. He wouldn't have wanted her to see what he was doing. It would only make her feel bad.

"I–I don't think so." He started to hand it back, embarrassment flushing his cheeks. "I've read everything in it that I wanted to."

There was another lie. Deep in his heart he knew that he wanted to keep it and read it over and over.

"Go ahead and keep it," Phil insisted.

"You might need it," Mack argued.

"I've got another one. I'll make you a present of this one."

Mack thanked him and shoved the Testament deep into his pocket and out of sight. He was glad that Phil had given it to him. He couldn't let anyone know how glad he was to have the book, but he was pleased about it. Now he could read some of those things for himself and try to figure out what they meant. With an air of affected casualness he sauntered back to the little house where he lived with his mother and brothers and sisters.

"How did you like what Mr. Roper said this morning?" Eduardo asked him as they sat down to dinner that noon.

"All right, I guess." Mack hoped the flames in his cheeks didn't show.

Eduardo stopped eating for an instant, his fork

poised in the air. "I don't think I'll go back to those meetings anymore."

Mamma nodded in agreement. "It is not good for any of us to go there. We have our religion. It is not good for us to change."

Mack didn't reply, but he wasn't sure he agreed with her either. He didn't like the idea of having their mother or anyone else tell him what he could do and what he couldn't do. He was the head of the house. He made the big decisions. It was not good for them to tell him he couldn't go to the Ropers to church if he wanted to.

* * *

Mack did keep going to Sunday school, but only to show his mother and Eduardo that they couldn't tell him what to do. He didn't go because he wanted to. It made him miserable most of the time.

For the next few weeks Mack continued to go to school and take care of his daily chores around the Circle-R ranch the same as always. In fact, he did a better job than he usually did. He cleaned out the barn, fixed a new hinge on the yard gate, and fed the calves without having to be told. The rancher couldn't figure out what had happened.

"I used to think Mack was a little careless about his work," Clarence Roper said at the supper table one evening, "but something has sure come over him. If he keeps on, he's going to be the best man on the place when he gets a little older."

Mack only grunted when Clarence said something to him about it. Let Mr. Roper think what he wanted to. He couldn't tell him the real reason that he was working so hard. When a guy was working he didn't think so much. It was the thinking that tormented him: thinking about God and Jesus Christ and the fact that he was a sinner and couldn't go to heaven. The harder he tried to keep such thoughts out of his mind the more they persisted in popping back.

He couldn't understand it. One minute he would be feeling great and the next he'd feel terrible. All it took was a chance remark by someone or a stray thought about what the Bible said, and he would get so upset that he could scarcely stand it.

At the oddest times, snatches of the songs they sang so often in Sunday school would come back to him. At other times he would remember some of the Bible verses he heard during the informal service. He didn't remember every word, but enough to cause the verses to bother him. Then there were the talks that Clarence Roper had given. For some reason they stuck with Mack more vividly than anything else.

The Mexican boy would never forget the morning the rancher told them how his own life was changed. He told them how he had always felt that he was able to take care of himself in any situation that came up.

It didn't make any difference what it was or how difficult it was, he figured he could handle it.

"I suppose most of the rest of you guys feel the same way," he said. "That's the kind of country we live in. We get used to taking care of ourselves."

Several of the ranchers there nodded understandingly. They too had that same feeling of self-sufficiency.

"I not only got to the place where I thought I didn't need God, I hated Him and anyone who tried to say anything to me about confessing my sin and letting Jesus Christ save me. I figured I didn't have to be saved. I was good enough, so I could get to heaven on my own." Mr. Roper paused significantly. "I didn't realize it then, but I was actually fighting God because I didn't want to do what He said I had to do if I was to be a Christian. The day came when I saw that I was only kidding myself, that I was headed for an eternity apart from God – an eternity in hell unless I confessed my sin and let Jesus Christ give me eternal life."

Listening, Mack realized that he was just like Clarence Roper had been. He had been hating God too. He still hated Him. He had gotten mad at anyone who tried to make him understand that he needed Jesus Christ.

"But I'm so thankful that my wife and son didn't give up on me," Clarence went on. "They kept praying for me and talking to me until I couldn't hold out any longer. I did just as I'm asking you to do now. I got down on my knees and told God what a sinner I was and that I was trusting Jesus Christ to save me. Now I'm happier than I've ever been in my life, and I know that when I die I will go to heaven."

Mack couldn't help wishing that he could be as happy as his employer. What Mr. Roper said was true. He had always been nice to Mack and his mother and the little ones, but he became so much nicer after he became a Christian. He didn't get mad like he used to, for one thing; and he didn't seem to be so interested in making money all the time.

It was easier for Phil and Mrs. Roper too. Mack knew that the rancher had been giving them a bad time. He supposed that was because they had been talking to him about becoming a Christian.

Mack felt a tug at his heart as he thought about the things that Clarence Roper was saying. He wanted to be a Christian, but something inside him kept fighting that desire – something that he didn't quite understand. All he knew was that he bristled whenever anyone talked that way to him.

At first he didn't even remember the New Testament he had hidden in the bottom of the box where he kept his clothes. When he left Sunday school the Sunday morning Phil gave him the Testament, he fully intended to read it. He even thought he would read it that afternoon, going over some of the verses Mr. Roper read to see if he could understand them a little better.

But he had his mother to think about. She hadn't liked it much when he started going to Sunday school. She would be terribly upset if she saw him reading the Bible. So he put it away the first chance he got so his mother wouldn't find it, and he had promptly forgotten it. It would probably have stayed deep in the box if the things Clarence said hadn't disturbed him so much. It was enough to drive a guy out of his mind.

"Get your Bibles out and read them," Mr. Roper would say practically every Sunday. "See for yourselves what God has to say to you about sin and how you can be sure that you are going to heaven."

Maybe that was the answer to his problem, Mack decided. He was going to get out that New Testament Phil had given him and read it. Only he would have to wait until he got a good chance. He couldn't have his mother or one of the little ones catch him at it.

He didn't know why, but from the moment he made up his mind to read the New Testament, it seemed that someone was always in the house. He took to slipping back to the house at odd times in an effort to find the place empty so he could get out his New Testament and read. Once, he went into the bedroom when no one else was home and got the book out of its hiding place; but before he could find the place Mr. Roper said to read, Eduardo came hurrying in to find him. It was almost a week later before he actually got a chance to start reading. His mother had gone over to the bunkhouse kitchen and was fixing supper. Eduardo was working with Phil and his dad, and the little ones were playing outside.

Mack looked about quickly to be sure that no one saw him, then slipped quickly into the house and made for the bedroom. Hurriedly he dug the Bible out and began to thumb through it.

He was surprised to find so many marks in the New Testament Phil had given him. He hadn't supposed that anyone would write in a holy Book. If he had one of his own, he wouldn't mark in it, he knew that right now.

But the marks weren't like the scribbling the little ones made in books. Some of the words had lines drawn under them as though they were words that Phil particularly wanted to remember. One of the verses Phil had underlined was one that Mack had heard Clarence Roper use a lot of times. Phil and Maria and some of the others knew it so well they didn't have to have their Bibles open to say it.

"For God so loved the world, that he gave his only begotten Son, that whosoever believeth in him should not perish, but have everlasting life."

Mack read it over two or three times slowly, pronouncing the words under his breath. He didn't know how Phil could stand to get up and say that verse. He could hardly read it to himself, the words drove so deeply into his heart.

He leafed through a number of pages until he

came to another verse that Phil had marked. That one seemed even worse to him.

"For the wages of sin is death; but the gift of God is eternal life through Jesus Christ our Lord."

Mack read the verse a second time. He knew well enough what it meant. It was talking about the lies he had told and the bad things he had done. He tried to make himself believe those things were just little things, but in his heart he knew that they weren't. They were sin, and that verse said that the wages of sin was death. It meant that he deserved to die.

The muscles in his throat tightened convulsively. And it was all he could do to keep from crying.

But there was more to that verse that made it sound a lot different. Mack didn't know for sure what it meant about Jesus Christ giving God's gift of eternal life, but he thought it must have something to do with the wages of sin being death.

As he thought about it, his spirits soared. Perhaps he wouldn't have to pay for his sin after all. Perhaps Clarence Roper was right when he said that God didn't want anyone to go to hell, but He wanted everyone to be in heaven with Him. The way Mack got it, that was the reason God had sent Jesus Christ to live on earth, to die on the cross, and be raised again.

He couldn't understand it, that was sure. He didn't see how confessing his sin and putting his trust in Jesus Christ would make him good enough to go to heaven, but Clarence Roper said that was the way it was, and the way those Bible verses sounded, Mack had to agree with him. Still, it bothered him when he couldn't understand how it could be.

He read the verses again, trying to figure out for sure what they meant. He should have heard his mother come into the house. A few moments before he had been listening for her, but now he was so concerned with what he was reading that he forgot all about her.

Then he heard the outside door open.

She was coming back to the house! He leaped to his feet and began to shove the Testament into the box of clothes, but he was too late. She had heard him in the bedroom and had hurried across the living room and flung open the door.

"Mack!" she cried. "What are you doing?"

He looked up, the color snaking up his neck and into his cheeks.

"I–I–" The lie that came into his mind would not leave his lips.

"What is that Book you have in your hand?" she demanded.

He knew by the tone that she had recognized it! His lithe young body suddenly lost its strength. She had caught him reading the New Testament! She knew!

CHAPTER 7

AN IMPOSSIBLE DEMAND

Silence hung tautly between them. Mack tried to speak, but the words clogged his throat. Scarlet surged to his face and fled, leaving his cheeks sallow. He moved, as though to hide the Testament behind him, but that wouldn't do either.

Mrs. Flores stepped closer to her frightened son, her piercing black eyes fixed on the Book he still held in his hand. She held her arms stiffly at her side and her thin lips tightened. She too found difficulty in speaking.

"What is that you are reading, Mack?" she wanted to know at last. The dismay and anger that mingled in her voice told him that she had no need to speak. She had already guessed the answer to her question and was stunned by it.

He did not move. How could he when such a thing was happening?

"What are you reading?" she asked again, imperiously, this time in a tone that demanded his reply. Mutely he held up the New Testament that Phil Roper had given him. He didn't want to show it to his mother, but he had no choice. She had caught him with it. Even lying to her now wouldn't do any good. She already knew what it was but was stunned to see him have it.

Mrs. Flores reached out nervously to take the Book from him but stopped suddenly, her fingers almost on it. She drew back, recoiling as though even touching the Testament would be wrong for her.

"No!" she cried, the word slipping, unbidden, from her lips.

"But it is not a bad Book, Mamma," he countered, desperately. "See, it is a *good* Book. It tells about Jesus Christ."

Her face was ashen and the worry lines about her mouth deepened. Suddenly she looked drained of strength and very, very old. It made Mack's heart ache to see her so disturbed.

"I know, but we do not read such a Book. I have told you that many times, Mack. The village elders forbid it."

This was something Mack could not understand. Why would it matter what the village elders said? They weren't back in Mexico now. They were in Texas. The elders wouldn't even know about the

Testament; and if they did, they could not tell Mack and his mother what to do.

"That Book is for the white man, the Yanqui. It is not for us. We are Mexican. We have our own gods."

Mack hesitated, trying to find words that would say what he felt in his heart.

"But Mr. Roper does not say it that way, Mamma," he began. "He says this book is not for the Yanqui alone. It is for the Mexican as well. He says this Book is for everyone. And he is a good man, Mamma. He would not lie to us."

She thought about that. Clarence Roper was a good man. What Mack said was true. And he had to believe what he said or he would not say it. She had never known him to lie to her or to anyone else. But the elders had been so strong in what they said about the evangelicals. It made her mind spin to think of it.

"Mr. Roper says that Jesus Christ died on the cross to save me – and you and the little ones."

"*Sí.*" She too had heard Senor Roper talk about such things many times in the last few months. She had attended his Sunday school more often than she wanted to go. She knew what he had said. But it was not the same as she had been taught when she was a girl back in their village in Mexico. There the elders forbade them to read the very Book her oldest son was now holding in his hand. And everyone knew that the elders were the wisest men in the village. It was always so. Her thoughts churned wildly as she tried to sort out the things Mack was saying and weigh them against the mature judgment of the elders.

At that moment she wished that Clarence Roper had not taken them in and given her a job. She wished that they had stayed back in Mexico. If they had, she wouldn't be faced with such a problem.

But Senor Roper had taken them in and had given her a job, and he had started the Sunday school that was causing all the trouble. She hadn't even wondered what the elders would say when the rancher invited them to Sunday school, nor when they had gone and heard him read and speak from the Book. But seeing her son have it in his hands brought back the old taboos with a rush.

"Is the Book yours?" She scarcely even dared to ask the question, but she had to know.

"It isn't mine." Mack spoke quickly. "It belongs to Phil Roper. He loaned it to me the other day. I have to give it back."

That made it a little better. If it didn't belong to Mack, it wouldn't be in the house all the time. He would be giving it back. She didn't think she could have stood it if the Testament had actually belonged to her son.

"If it belongs to him, take it back to him!" Her voice was harsh and rasping. "It is not good for you to have that Book in our house. It is not good for any of us!"

Mack studied her face seriously. This was not a

request; it was an order. It was the first time since Papa died that she had told him he had to do something.

"You understand? You take it back!"

He cringed. She sounded as though she was scolding one of the little ones. If she hadn't been so angry, it would have made him furious to be treated so. After all, he was the man of the house. She had told him so herself. Why should he have to take orders from her like Eduardo or the others?

"All right, all right," he said, "If you feel that way about it, I'll give it back to him, Mamma."

"That is the way I feel. I don't want that Book in this house another minute!"

"I only brought it into the house so I can put it away good where it won't be torn or lost. I'll give it back to him right away."

That seemed to please her slightly. She relaxed and managed a weak smile. "And you won't read it anymore, Mack?" she asked.

He did not answer her. Why did she think she could tell him what he could read? He was big enough and old enough to take care of the family. He was a man.

His mother took his silence to mean that he agreed to do what she said. She stepped forward quickly and kissed him on the forehead.

"You are a good boy, Mack," she said impulsively. "You do what Mamma asks you to."

He looked quickly away. He wanted to do what she said, but why should he? Papa didn't have to mind her and he was taking Papa's place. Besides, this was different. He felt a pull that he had not known before.

What could there be in that New Testament that would make the elders and his mother so anxious that he not read it? What was it they were afraid he would find out?

"You take the Book over to the ranch house and give it back to Phil while I get supper, Mack. OK?"

"You mean I have to take it right away?" He was going to take it back. He couldn't see why she was getting so anxious about it.

"The little ones might find it," Mamma explained weakly. "And if they did, they might insist that we read it to them. That would not be good. That would not be good at all."

Mack shifted the Testament to his left hand and shuffled towards the door. He didn't know what he would tell Phil when he took the Testament back to him. Phil had insisted that he keep it. Mamma said that it wouldn't be good to read the Testament to the little ones, but it wouldn't be good to take a gift back to someone, either. Especially someone who was as good a friend as Phil Roper. Phil would think he didn't want it.

Besides, what his mother said had only made him the more curious about what was actually in the New Testament. He had been interested because of what Clarence Roper said in Sunday school and some of the things that Phil had told him, but this was different. Why would the elders in their village back home be so afraid of this Book? If he did as she wanted him to do, he would never find out.

Halfway to the ranch house Mack paused. If he hid the Book somewhere, his mother would never know the difference. All he had to do was lie to her when she asked him if he had given the Book back to Phil. She was much too shy to ask Phil about it herself. That way he could read the Book for a while and find out for himself why everybody was so against his reading it.

Impulsively Mack turned and made his way to the barn. The sun had set an hour before and darkness was shrouding the ranch, but Mack did not hesitate. He had been in the barn countless times at night. He could move quickly in the darkness.

Just inside the door he stopped. He wouldn't have to worry about his mother finding the Testament out in the barn. That was one place she never went. But he had to hide it in a place where Clarence Roper or Phil would not find it.

The old saddlebags! There wasn't a better place to hide something on the whole ranch. Those saddle-bags had probably been hanging on the same peg for twenty-five years. No one would ever think to look there.

Groping, he found the bags, opened one flap and carefully put the Testament in the bag. A few moments later he was back at the house.

His mother frowned when she saw him. "You are back so soon, Mack?" she asked.

He nodded, trying to keep her from seeing the color that was staining his cheeks.

"I thought we'd be ready to eat soon."

"*Sí*." She turned back to the stove to tend to the tortillas. "But, Mack, how come you got so dirty? There was no dust on your hands and face when you went over to the Roper house."

His temper flared. "How should I know? I did what you wanted me to do, Mamma. I thought you would be satisfied."

"*Sí*." It makes me happy that you do what I ask, Mack," she said, "but I wonder about the dirt on your face. I wouldn't want them to think I let you go dirty."

There it was again. She ordered him to do one thing and now she was talking about something else, as though she was responsible for his being dirty. He was glad that he had hidden the Testament instead of giving it back to Phil. She wasn't going to run *him*, that was for sure.

* * *

In the ranch house that evening, the Roper family had just finished dinner but were lingering at the table for devotions. Phil went into the living room and got the family Bible. Clarence took it and opened it to the marker that indicated the place where they had been reading.

"I think it's your turn, Maria," he said, handing the leatherbound Book to his daughter. "We're starting with Romans ten."

Her smile flashed. "You didn't have to tell me where to start reading. I remembered."

They settled back and listened while she read. When she finally finished, it was time for them to go to prayer. The rancher took over, as was his custom.

"Before we start, do any of you have anything special that you would like to have us pray about tonight?"

There was a short silence.

"I do," Phil said. "I think we ought to pray for Mack again." He told them about giving the Testament to his young friend.

"He should be on our daily prayer list," Carmen put in. "And we ought to pray for his mother too. I've been quite burdened for her."

Maria nodded. "And for his brothers and sisters," she added. "They need Jesus, too."

Clarence Roper took a small notebook from his pocket and thumbed it to a blank page where he jotted down the names of the Flores family. He had written them down on something once before, but he had misplaced it. Now he wrote them down again.

"I've got a confession to make," he said. "I promised you that I would pray for Mack in my personal prayers, Phil. I did for a while, but I started to neglect it and for about the last month I've completely forgotten to pray for him."

"I've been forgetting to pray for him once in a while myself," Phil added. "But lately I've been thinking an awful lot about him. He acts as though he wants to take a stand for Christ."

"That sounds wonderful. I didn't realize you'd had much of a chance to talk to him."

"I haven't talked to him much, but sometimes he acts like he wants to become a Christian and the next time it seems as if something is holding him back."

Mr. Roper thought about that for a moment. "Satan is going to fight his making a decision with every tool he can command." He paused significantly. "I know. That's what happened to me. I used to think I'd about as soon be dead as to let Christ have complete control of my life."

There were two or three other prayer requests before the Roper family went to prayer. Each one prayed in turn, beginning with Maria and ending with Carmen. They asked God to bless them and to help them in their efforts to reach their neighbors and friends for Christ through the Sunday school. Phil prayed for Mack Flores, and Maria prayed for the rest of the Mexican family, praying for each one.

CHAPTER 8

NEW PLANS

Spring was coming to the parched Texas prairies. The pastures were beginning to green and the trees were budding. The calves were already arriving, and Clarence Roper and his cowhands were busier than ever. But, for all of the work there was to do around the Circle-R, there was a new topic of conversation, a topic that excited all the family.

Clarence mentioned it one evening after they had finished praying for Mack and his mother and the younger children.

"What's Mack's reaction to the gospel now, Phil?" he asked. "Have you had a chance to talk to him?"

The boy nodded. "I tried a couple of times, Dad, but to tell you the truth I couldn't get very far with him. He acts as though he's afraid of something."

"Maybe he is," Mrs. Roper added knowingly. "I

know how hard it is for him to accept Christ with the opposition that he would have."

Phil breathed deeply. "I wish Doug and Del were going to be here this summer. They'd be able to do a lot better job of talking to him than I would." Clarence toyed with his ballpoint pen, thoughtfully. It was a full minute before he spoke. "Well now, I don't suppose that would be too hard to arrange."

His son's eyes widened. "Do you mean what I think you mean, Dad?"

"I don't know what you think I mean." Amusement danced in his eyes. "But I've been thinking that maybe we ought to invite them down here for a while this summer." He looked up at his wife. "What do you say about it, honey? Would you like that?"

She managed a crooked little smile. "It would be nice, I guess."

Maria and Phil groaned inwardly. She hadn't sounded very excited about it. Maybe she didn't want them around. Maybe she thought it would be too much work or something.

"You don't sound very enthusiastic about it," Clarence told her.

"Oh, it isn't that I don't want them. I'd love to have them come. It's just that I've been thinking a lot about taking Maria and going up to Minnesota to visit the triplets and Danny and Kay this summer. I thought I'd like to go on up to the Angle to see Carl and Mary Orlis."

Maria broke in. "I've been telling Mother how nice it is up where Uncle Carl and Aunt Mary live. And I'd like to see Blackie. He's Del's pet crow that talks. And I'd want to have Mother meet Barney, the old Indian man; and we could see the horses we gave to DeeDee and Del and Doug and–"

Phil was still unconvinced. "That'd be a lot of fun, but I still think it would be a lot better if they'd come down here. Think of all the things we could do, and they could get next to Mack too and maybe lead him to Christ."

For several minutes Phil and Maria argued about it, in brother-sister fashion. At last Phil turned to their father.

"There's only one way to settle this and still satisfy everybody, Dad. We'll have to send Mom and Maria up to Minnesota and have the boys come down here."

Maria jerked her head saucily. "Now, that would just suit me fine. I'd be able to get away from you for a little while."

Phil had only been teasing when he suggested that the family split up for their vacations that year. He didn't think that their folks would go for his mother and Maria taking off for Minnesota while Doug and Del came down to the ranch to visit him and his dad. But the more they talked about it, the more practical it seemed to be. Surprisingly, Clarence Roper agreed with the plan.

"It would give you a chance to visit with Kay,

Carmen," Mr. Roper said, "while Maria and DeeDee are together. And Phil and I could entertain the boys."

She considered the matter carefully. At first the idea sounded preposterous. There would have to be someone at the ranch to cook and clean and wash for Clarence and the boys. And she didn't like the thought of going off with just her daughter, even if it was only to be for a short visit. She liked to have the whole family together as much as possible. But the more she thought about it, the more practical it seemed.

"Mack's mother would be here to cook and clean for you and the boys," she said. "That's one thing I wouldn't have to worry about."

Phil's eyes gleamed. "Then we can have Doug and Del come down for a while?" he asked. "It's all right with you, Mom?"

His dad spoke up. "We'll have to write first and see how this sort of thing fits in with their plans. They might have something else in mind."

But Phil was confident that everything was going to work out. "We don't have to worry about that. They'll come down for the summer. I know they will."

His mother smiled. "If I didn't know you better, Philip, I'd think you want to get rid of me."

Mack didn't get much opportunity to read the New Testament he had secreted in the old saddlebags hanging in the barn. There was little danger that his mother would catch him with it, but it seemed that

Eduardo or Phil or Mr. Roper or one of the hands was always popping in at the wrong time.

"Hi, Mack," Clarence Roper said on one occasion when he caught him in the barn. "What are you doing, taking a little nap or hiding from your mother?"

The ranch owner was only joking, but Mack didn't take it that way. "I–I just came out here for–for–" The words choked in his throat. What could a guy go out to the barn for? "I came out for my jacket."

Clarence looked about curiously. "I don't see any jacket here."

"I–I must have left it someplace else." With that he backed to the door. "Good-bye, Mr. Roper, I've got to run. I think maybe Mamma is looking for me."

He turned and dashed in the direction of the house, his Testament thrust deeply into his pocket. He was almost at the kitchen door when he remembered it. Now what was he going to do? She'd see it for sure.

Mack turned off uneasily and went out behind the bunkhouse where he stayed until he saw Mr. Roper go back to the house. Then he scurried to the barn and returned the Testament to its hiding place.

Some of the things he read that afternoon drummed ceaselessly in his mind. God hadn't sent Jesus Christ into the world to condemn the world, He sent Him so people could be saved and go to heaven. At least that was what Mack thought that verse meant. He had read it over a dozen times and that was the only thing that made sense to him. Still, he wondered how

God could have loved him enough to have sent His own Son to die on the cross for *him*. If he'd been good – even a little bit good – it might be true. But he hadn't. He'd done all sorts of bad things. There wasn't anything about him that would make God want to save him. Again that night Mack didn't sleep.

The next Sunday morning he got up a little earlier than usual and put on his best clothes. His mother watched him nervously.

"Are you going to Sunday school today, no?" she asked with growing uneasiness.

He hesitated. Before going out to read that Book he had thought he was through with Sunday school, but the last couple of days he had been trying to make up his mind about it. One minute he thought he would go and the next he was sure that it was best to stay at home.

"Phil asked me to go with him this morning," he alibied.

"You can tell him no," she retorted. "You can tell him that your mamma doesn't want you to go."

His eyes flashed. There she went again! He didn't know why she had to keep on talking that way. She acted as though he was suddenly younger than Eduardo and she had to watch everything he did.

"I told him that I'd go with him this morning," he said firmly.

Tears came to her eyes, and for an instant he wavered, almost weakening.

"There is no harm in going as long as I don't listen to what Mr. Roper says."

"But you *might* listen," she said, desperation creeping into her voice. "You *might* listen!"

He walked away quickly.

Mack sat at the table with the rest of the family for breakfast that morning, but he said nothing to his mother or the little ones. Mrs. Flores said nothing either, and two or three times she wiped a tear from her eyes. Eduardo noticed it and wanted to find out what was wrong, but she wouldn't tell him.

"It is nothing," she said, trying to smile. "It is all over now. Poof! It is forgotten."

Mack was watching his younger brother. Eduardo said no more, but it was obvious that he knew there was something wrong between Mack and Mamma. As soon as Mack finished eating, he got up from the table and hurried outside. He had to get out of sight quickly, he realized. Eduardo would not be far behind him.

His younger brother did come out looking for him. Mack, who ducked around the corner of the house, watched him leave the little porch, take a few steps in the direction of the barn and stop to look about uncertainly. He came over presently and looked around the corner, but Mack had seen him start in that direction and managed to get out of sight.

A few minutes before Sunday school, Mack sauntered across the ranch yard to the Roper home. Most of the people had already arrived and were sitting in small clusters, visiting quietly. Mack slipped in and sat down. He knew that Phil would be looking for him, but he didn't want to see him if he could help it. He wanted to be able to sit near the door so he could get out when he wanted to.

The meeting was much the same as the others. Again Mr. Roper talked about the fact that everyone needed to confess his sin and put his trust in Christ to go to heaven. He quoted some Bible verses, but Mack didn't have the Testament along so he could not look them up. He frowned and stared uneasily at the floor.

Mr. Roper didn't need to think that he was going to snare *him* with all that talk about everyone being a sinner and needing a Savior. That was all right for those that wanted it, but he wasn't buying any.

Even if he wanted to, he wouldn't. He wasn't going to hurt his mother by doing anything like becoming a Christian. He hadn't realized she was so opposed to it until she caught him with the Bible in his hands. He didn't know what would happen to her if he ever made a decision for Christ.

The tall rancher continued to talk quietly, telling about a stranger he had met not long before.

"I tried to talk with him about Jesus Christ and his need of having a personal relationship with Him, but he wouldn't listen to me. He ordered me to stop talking to him." There was a pained silence as he paused, looking from one sober face to another. "Before the week was out, he was in an accident on the highway and died before they got him to the hospital. I felt terrible about it, but you know, it wasn't my fault. I had talked with him about his need of Jesus Christ. He had his chance to go to heaven and rejected it. Now, it's too late."

Mack Flores squirmed with growing discomfort. He wished he had listened to his mother when she tried to get him to stay home that morning. He'd feel a lot better if he had.

He didn't know why Mr. Roper had to talk that way. He ought to know that the only thing he could do was to make people mad. Mack wouldn't have been surprised if everybody had gotten up and stormed out after he talked like that. No one could have blamed them. That was what Mack really wanted to do.

The rancher opened his Bible once more and began to read some verses that said that those who "believed on Jesus" would be saved, and those who didn't would be lost. That shook Mack more than he had been shaken in a long while. He knew well enough which group he was in. The Bible made that clear. He was one of the lost.

He couldn't stand it!

Abruptly, the boy jumped to his feet and stormed out, slamming the door behind him. Mr. Roper didn't need to think that he could talk to him any way he wanted to and have him sit and take it. And what was more, he wasn't going to go back and listen to that stuff again.

Mack was halfway across the ranch yard when the door he just came out of opened once more. He heard it close and turned quickly, startled to see Phil striding toward him. His cheeks crimsoned and for an instant his hands trembled.

"Hi, Mack. I didn't know you were at the service this morning. I looked for you, but I didn't see you come in."

He looked about as though trying frantically to find some way of escape. But there was none. He had to stay there and face Phil.

His friend stopped beside him.

"What did you think of the lesson this morning?" he asked. There was nothing in his voice to indicate that he realized how angry Mack was.

The youth shrugged with exaggerated indifference. "It was all right, I guess, if you go for that junk."

Phil winced. "Did you understand what Dad was talking about?"

The muscles in the other boy's body stiffened convulsively. "No, I didn't. And I didn't want to, either! I've had it with that kind of talk!"

CHAPTER 9

GREAT NEWS AND BAD NEWS

The days lagged endlessly from sun to sun for Mack Flores. He had a certain number of odd jobs around the Circle-R that he did mechanically, not because he wanted to, but because they were his responsibility. And he went to school with Phil, Maria, and Eduardo the same as always.

At first he was wary of being around Phil, especially if the two of them happened to be alone together. He suspected that his friend might try to bring up the subject of Sunday school and that religion of his, and Mack steeled himself against it. That was one thing he wasn't going to allow to happen. He'd watch when Phil started to maneuver the conversation and get it sidetracked. He wasn't going to be preached to again.

Surprisingly, however, Phil did not mention the incident to him again. Nor did he try to get Mack to talk about spiritual things with him. As far as Mack was concerned, things were just as they had been before Phil got high on religion. They went on as though nothing had come between them. Although the older boy seemed to have completely forgotten what happened, the younger boy thought of little else. He wished he could go back to that morning and change the things he had said to Phil. He was sorry he had lost his temper and jumped on him the way he had. The rancher's son was his very best friend, there was no doubt of that.

In spite of the fact that Phil didn't seem to be upset, Mack was disturbed by his own outburst. He didn't know why Mr. Roper's talk that morning had bothered him so much. Or why it still bothered him, for that matter.

But it did. His mind kept going back to the rancher's talk. He shuddered as he remembered those Bible verses. They spelled only condemnation for him because he could not confess his sin and become a Christian – not with his mother being so bitterly opposed to it.

And that even made things worse. It wasn't long until he had difficulty in sleeping at night and could think of little else during the day. He had reason to be mad at Mr. Roper and at Phil and the rest of the family. If it weren't for them he wouldn't be so upset.

It really wasn't his fault that he was so disturbed, he decided. It was that religion of theirs that caused all of the trouble. He had gotten so worked up over it that he scarcely knew what he was doing.

There was one thing he had learned, though. He wasn't going back to that Sunday school anymore.

* * *

Mrs. Flores watched Mack carefully to see if he was being influenced by the Sunday school and the New Testament she had caught him with.

"What is it that's bothering you?" she would ask nervously. "You do not smile all week."

"I'm all right," he replied.

"Are you thinking you would like to go back to Mexico?" she asked. "Are you lonesome for our old village?"

He shook his head. Why would he be lonely for their village? All he could remember about it was that they were hungry most of the time and hardly had clothes to wear. No, things were much better in Texas, especially on the Circle-R. He didn't like the things Mr. Roper and his family were saying to him, and he hated the Sunday school, but he did appreciate the fact that there was always plenty of food to eat, and they had a nice house and clothes. He had no desire to go back to Mexico.

"If you like to go back, Mack," she continued, "we can go. Maybe it would be better for us there now."

"No!" The word lashed out. "It is much better that we stay here."

She thought about that seriously. What Mack said was true. Life had been much easier for her and the children since they had come to the Circle-R. Just thinking about leaving made her heart ache. But she did not like to see her oldest son so sad. And she could not bear the thought that he might decide to walk the way of the Ropers' religion. That would be even worse than going back to their old home in the mountains of northern Mexico.

"You aren't going back to that Sunday school, are you, Mack?"

Anger flared suddenly in his eyes. "I won't go back there anymore!" he exclaimed vehemently.

Mrs. Flores sighed her relief. "You are a good boy, Mack. You do what Mamma wants you to do."

* * *

Phil and Maria Roper were watching the mail closely as the time when they should be hearing from the triplets and Danny and Kay Orlis drew near. They raced over to the mailbox as soon as the bus let them out at the lane to see if a letter from Minnesota had come yet. Phil got there first by just a step. Maria tried to crowd him aside but didn't quite succeed.

"Is there anything for me from DeeDee?" she demanded eagerly.

"How should I know?" He thumbed the envelopes with a tantalizing deliberation that made her furious.

"You don't have to take all day, do you?"

"Here." He thrust the letters into her hands. "If you're in such a big hurry, don't let me stop you. Go ahead. Look for yourself."

He had already checked the day's mail and satisfied himself that there was nothing there for him.

Now he was making her do the same. Maria stuck her tongue out at him. Most of the time he was nice, but there were times when he was contemptible. She didn't know why big brothers had to be so–so– She couldn't even find the word that described him.

A moment or two later she had looked through the mail and had seen that there was no mail for either of them.

"They didn't write to us," she said, making no effort to hide her disappointment. "And there's been plenty of time for us to get a letter."

They started up the long lane to the ranch house.

"I sure thought that we would be hearing from Doug and Del by this time," Phil said. "Usually they get a letter right back to us, especially when we write about something so important."

"And I thought I'd have a letter from DeeDee today. I'm beginning to wonder if Kay and DeeDee really want Mother and me to come up and see them."

Phil shrugged. He knew what his sister meant. He was beginning to wonder whether the boys wanted to come south and spend some time on the Circle-R with him and his dad. At first he had looked forward confidently to their coming, sure that they would be as anxious to come down to the ranch for three or four weeks as he and Dad were to have them. But now it had been so long since his dad had invited them that Phil was beginning to doubt whether they even wanted to come.

Maybe they had other plans for the summer. That could very well be. They usually did something special like hitching a ride with Danny when he went somewhere interesting to fly for the mission. Or maybe they just didn't want to come to Texas to visit.

"Maybe they aren't coming, Maria."

Her pretty young face darkened. "It'll just ruin everything if Kay and DeeDee don't want Mother and me to come up to Minnesota to visit them."

"It'd be worse if the boys didn't want to come down here."

She wrinkled her nose at him again. That was the way with boys! The things they did were always more important than anything anyone else wanted to do.

When they got to the house their mother rifled through the mail and extracted a letter from Kay. "I thought you said that we didn't hear from them."

Both Phil and Maria gasped in surprise and pushed close to her. "Did we get a letter? Do they want to come?"

Carmen's laughter rippled. "Just give me time to open it and we'll all find out," she told them.

Phil waited tensely, watching their mother's face as she read the short letter. "Does she want you to come?" he demanded. "Are the boys going to come down here to see Dad and me?"

After a moment Carmen looked up. "Kay sounds as excited about all of this as we are."

Maria squealed gleefully. "Oh, that's wonderful!"

"I'll say it is," Phil retorted. "I won't have to put up with you for a while." He tried to sound serious, but he didn't deceive anyone, not even Maria. She laughed at him.

"Big deal! It's going to be a real relief for me too. Don't forget that. I won't have to put up with you either."

* * *

Mack wasn't quite sure what turned his thinking back to the Book that Phil had given him. He figured that was one chapter in his life that was closed, that he would never go out to the barn and look at it again. He would have given it back to Phil if he hadn't been afraid of hurting his friend. Let him think that he had the Testament in the house and that he might get it out and read it sometime. There wasn't any harm in that.

He might have forgotten the New Testament he

had hidden in the barn had it not been for his mother and Eduardo. It was all their fault that things happened the way they did.

"It is so good you no longer have that Book, Mack," she said at the supper table. "It is such a relief to me that you took it back to Senor Roper's boy."

"What book?" Eduardo demanded.

Mack knew that crimson was staining his cheeks, and he looked down at the table.

"It was just a book," he mumbled into his plate.

"What book, Mamma?" Eduardo persisted.

"One of those Books that Senor Roper reads from in Sunday school and talks about," she said, "a–a Bible."

Eduardo's gaze came up impishly to meet Mack's. "Maybe he didn't give it back, Mamma. Maybe he's still got it hidden somewhere."

Mack winced. What did his younger brother know? Why did he say such a thing? Had he found the Testament in the old saddlebag? Had he seen him put it there?

"Maybe *you've* got one of those Books yourself," he muttered.

Mrs. Flores was worried. "What do you mean, Eduardo? Does Mack still have the Book?"

"He doesn't mean anything," the older boy blurted. "He's just trying to get me in trouble, that's all."

"Hush up!" She turned to Eduardo. "Does Mack still have the Book?"

Eduardo hesitated as though trying to make up his mind whether to continue or not.

"Does he?"

"He knows I don't. He just wants to make you mad at me, that's all."

That did it.

"Is that so? I know where there's one of those Books hidden, Mamma, and it's got Phil's name in it!"

Mack gasped! Eduardo *did* know! The strength fled from his legs, leaving him weak and trembling.

"That doesn't mean anything," he tried to lie. "It belongs to Phil."

"Mack!" His mother was furious.

"You can ask him if you want to!"

"I don't have to ask him! I would know that Book if I see it again!"

He glared helplessly at his younger brother. Just wait until this was over and he caught Eduardo out behind the barn alone. He'd wish he hadn't opened his big fat mouth about him!

"Get the light, Eduardo!" Mamma ordered sternly. "We will go out and see if this is the same Book that Mack was going to give back to Phil."

"Go ahead," Mack blustered. "Go on, if you don't believe me!"

She turned to face him, anger flashing in her eyes. "You come along!" she snapped.

The little ones would all have come too, following some distance behind, but Mamma ordered them back into the house. They did as they were told. Never had they seen their mother half so angry. It was enough to frighten anyone.

She walked between her two sons to the barn, half a step behind them as though afraid one or the other would scurry away. But she did not need to take that precaution. They both were afraid of her, so angry was she at that moment.

Just inside the barn she stopped. "All right, Eduardo!" her voice rasped, "Show me the Book!"

"Give me the light."

"Tell me where to shine it!"

He directed her attention to the far wall where the saddlebag was hanging and strode over to it.

"Here it is."

She stared at the Book, horror gleaming in her eyes.

"Mack! How could you do this thing?"

Before he could answer, she spun on her heel and slapped him savagely on the side of the head, knocking him against the manger. Then, as though it was all part of the same motion, she moved forward quickly, snatched the New Testament out of Eduardo's hands and began to rip it to pieces, throwing the pages wildly about the barn.

"Mamma!" Eduardo cried. "Don't!"

"You won't disobey me again with this Book, Mack!" she exclaimed. "I have seen to that!"

Mack straightened slowly, rubbing his face where the blow had fallen. He knew the imprint of her hand would stand out on his cheek, but that was nothing compared to the blow that struck his heart. It was as though something inside of him had died with his mother's slap. For the first time in years he felt like crying. He couldn't understand it, but he wasn't even mad at Eduardo anymore. He wasn't mad at anybody. He just wanted to get away where he could be alone with his misery.

CHAPTER 10

EDUARDO'S NEW SELF

The following Monday morning Doug and Del Davis received the check Clarence sent them so they could visit the Circle-R. They were trying to make up their minds when to get airline reservations to leave Minneapolis, when Danny was called on to fly to southern Mexico for the mission.

"I was just looking on the map," he said, "and it wouldn't be too far out of the way for me to take you right to the ranch. How does that sound to you guys?"

They both grinned. "Sounds great to us," Doug told him. "We'd much rather fly with you than on a commercial airline."

"You can say that again," his brother put in.

But DeeDee wasn't so sure. "Aunt Carmen and Maria are flying to Minneapolis, and we were supposed to pick them up the same day we took Doug and Del over to catch their plane. How are we going to work that?"

Danny laughed. "We'll leave that to you and Kay. You can go over and pick them up, can't you?"

"I'd never thought of that."

Danny and the boys took off in the early morning mists and by the time most people were having breakfast they were angling down to refuel at a small airport in Iowa. The boys went into the airport cafe and ordered breakfast for themselves and Danny while he supervised the refueling. He was one of those careful pilots who always double-checked every procedure to be sure that nothing was left undone. It wasn't often that he caught anything amiss; but on the few times that he had, there could have been serious problems.

Once the refueling was completed and Danny was satisfied that everything was in order, he went in and had breakfast. It wasn't long until they were in the air once more.

* * *

Eduardo was greatly disturbed as he and Mack and their mother went back to the house. He wished now that he hadn't told on Mack. He really hadn't intended to. In fact, when he saw the handprints in the dust on the old saddlebag and investigated, he thought the Testament must belong to Phil. It hadn't even occurred to him that his older brother could have put it there.

He remembered how he had laughed inwardly when he found it. Phil must have been a terrible fanatic, he decided, if he had to have a Bible out in the barn too. If he had dared, he would have teased him about it. And then Mamma started talking about the Book that Mack had; and without thinking, he had begun to taunt his brother. Even then he hadn't realized that Mack was the one who actually hid it there. Now he had gotten her upset and Mack in trouble. He wished that Mamma had slapped him instead of his brother. He was the one at fault.

Once in the house Mack made his way straight to the bedroom and shut the door tightly behind him.

"Isn't Mack going to eat?" one of the girls asked hesitantly.

Mamma scowled. "He'll finish supper after a while. Now hurry and eat so we can get the dishes done."

Eduardo only toyed with his food. He had gone to Sunday school once in a while, but he hadn't really listened to what had been said. It had simply been someplace for him to go; someplace where he could meet some of the guys from the surrounding ranches.

Now he wished that he had listened. There was something about all of this that gripped him and would not let go. He couldn't understand what there was about that Book that would make Mamma so mad at Mack for having it. He couldn't remember that she had ever slapped Mack before. She did punish the little ones occasionally, but she always said that Mack was the man of the house. She was different with him.

And what was there in that New Testament that would make Mack want to keep it after she had ordered him to give it back to Phil? He had always been obedient and was concerned about Eduardo and the little ones minding what Mamma said. It wasn't like him to disobey her.

It must be that the Book had something most important in it. That *had* to be the answer.

Before Eduardo finished supper that night, he had decided that he had to see for himself what was in the New Testament Mamma had torn apart and scattered about the barn. She might get mad and slap him for it if she found out. She might even take a switch to him, but he had to run that risk. He had to see for himself what was so important about that Testament that both Mamma and Mack were so upset about it.

As soon as supper was over, Eduardo went into the bedroom where his older brother was and got the flashlight. Mack was lying motionless on the bed.

"Mack," he whispered.

No answer.

"Mack. Mack."

He rolled over. "Go away and leave me alone."

"I'm sorry I got you in trouble with Mamma. I didn't mean to."

"A lot of good that does now." Anger and dismay mingled in his voice. "Just go on and leave me alone."

Eduardo stood motionless for an instant, trying to think of something to say. Then he tucked the flashlight under his sweater and slipped out.

"Where are you going, Eduardo?" Mamma demanded.

"I'll be back in a little while."

"See that you do!"

When he left the house the barn was his destination, but he did not go directly there. He turned and angled in the general direction of the bunkhouse. If Mamma was looking out the window, it would be better for her to see him going there than to the barn where the Testament lay scattered on the hay. If she knew what he was about, she would get after him the way she had Mack.

Once on the far side of the bunkhouse he turned and sped down to the barn. By this time only a few stars and a thin sliver of moon fought against the darkness, but Eduardo did not dare switch on the flashlight until he was safe inside and had the door tightly closed behind him. Then, frantically, he began to pick up the torn leaves of the Testament.

He stuffed them into his pocket and, taking one last look to be sure that he had gotten all of them, turned off the flashlight and left the barn.

He started to go back to the house but changed his mind and went to the ranch pickup instead. With a quick look around to see if he was being followed, he got inside. Using the dome light, he began to read the torn Testament.

At first it didn't make sense to him, all the talk about sin and being born again and getting a new life. Jesus Christ had something to do with all of that, he could tell that much; but he couldn't quite figure it all out. He paused thoughtfully, wondering if Mack understood it. He'd like to talk with him and see, but he didn't quite dare.

The thing that puzzled Eduardo the most was Mamma's attitude toward the Book. He sure hadn't read anything that would help him to understand why she was so opposed to it. It sounded as though it was something that she ought to read too, as well as he and Mack. And then there were the little ones. If what this Book said was true, they all ought to have this new life the Book talked about.

He was so interested in reading that he wanted to stay out there for at least half an hour, but he didn't dare. If he stayed too long, Mamma would be out after him. And he didn't want that. He found another hiding place for the New Testament under the pickup seat and went back to the house. He wanted to tell Mack that his Book wasn't gone, that he had hidden it for him; but his brother wouldn't listen. And he didn't know that he blamed him. Eduardo tossed restlessly half the night before finally drifting off to sleep.

* * *

Danny Orlis flew to the Circle-R ranch and landed in the north pasture near the buildings. Clarence Roper and Phil hadn't gotten back from taking Carmen and Maria to the airport, but Mack and Eduardo and the little ones came out to meet the aircraft. Doug spotted them before the plane came to a stop.

"There's Mack!" He waved vigorously.

Their Mexican friend saw the wave and returned it with enthusiasm.

"I'd almost forgotten about Mack and Eduardo," Del said. "It's sure going to be good to see them."

As Danny jumped down out of the aircraft, Mack approached. "You are Mr. Orlis?" he asked, holding out his hand.

"That's right."

"Mr. Roper told me that you might come before he and Phil got back."

"I suppose they're on their way home from the airport."

Mack nodded. "Yes, they should be home in a short time. But Mr. Roper told me I should help you tie down the plane for the night and have you go into the house and make yourself at home."

"Thanks, Mack," Danny said warmly. "We'll sure do that."

Mack turned his back on them and directed his attention to the task ahead. He wanted to talk to the boys. He remembered them from two years before when he and his mother and Eduardo and the little ones first came to the southern Texas ranch. But Mr. Roper had given him a job to do. He had trusted him. And if Mack wanted more jobs of trust, he knew that he had to take care of this one well. He had to see that Mr. Orlis's plane was tied down so a sudden Texas wind would not damage it and that the rancher's guest was in the house sitting in a comfortable chair. Then he could take time to talk with Doug and Del, but not until then.

Eduardo, who had been given no responsibility by the rancher, was there, nevertheless. He helped Danny and his older brother with the tie-down and waited beside Mack while Danny got a small duffel bag from the luggage compartment.

"I can carry it for you," Eduardo offered.

But Mack spoke up quickly. "No! It is for me to carry the bag. I am supposed to help Mr. Roper's guest."

Danny, who had started for the house with the bag in his hand, stopped and handed it to Mack. "Here," he said quietly. "You can carry it for me."

The boy's grin was as broad as his face. "You follow me. I'll take you to the house and help you get comfortable."

Eduardo tagged along, a few paces behind. He wished he could help the way Mack was doing, but

Mr. Roper had not given him that responsibility. All he could do was go along and watch.

Mack showed Danny into the house and insisted that he sit down in the living room.

"You watch the news on TV," he said, "or maybe you want to shave. You make yourself at home, Mr. Orlis."

"Fine. I'll do that."

"And Mamma will come over and fix you and Del and Doug something to eat."

Satisfied that he had taken care of everything Mr. Roper had asked him to, Mack went back to help the boys carry their luggage up to the house. His younger brother joined them.

"It sure is good to see you guys," Del said. "We've been doing a lot of thinking about you and wondering how you've been getting along."

"Yes, I work for Mr. Roper." Mack cocked his head proudly.

Eduardo cringed and wished he could say the same thing. He had asked the rancher about working for him often enough, but he had always said he was too young. Eduardo knew the time would come when he would be able to work on the ranch, but that didn't help him at the moment.

"And so does Mamma," Mack added proudly. "She does the cooking for the hands."

Doug spoke up. "You guys will have time to go

riding with us once in a while now that school's out, won't you?"

Eduardo would have answered right away, but not Mack. He had to think about that. He liked Doug and Del almost as much as he liked Phil, but he didn't know whether he wanted to be with three of them or not. It was hard enough being with Phil when he started talking to him about sin and his need of taking Christ as his Savior and things like that; he didn't know how he could stand it if he had to listen to three of them.

"I don't know," Mack replied. "Sometimes Mr. Roper keeps me awful busy."

* * *

Mack left the ranch house when Mrs. Flores did after cooking supper for the guests; but Eduardo stayed, sitting in the corner of the spacious kitchen. He didn't have much to say, except when they asked him a question; but he did like to listen to them. And when Danny got his Bible from his duffle bag and began to read from it, Eduardo scooted his chair as close as possible, hanging on to each word.

Danny didn't say where he was reading from and Eduardo didn't dare ask him, but it was a story about a guy who killed Christians. He was going someplace else after other Christians to kill them too, when a bright light made him blind.

Eduardo was glad of that. He got just what he deserved. It would have served him right if God had killed him too. But that wasn't what happened. They took him to a man who lived in a little house in the city. He prayed for him and God let him see again.

Danny stopped reading there, and Eduardo groaned inwardly. He wanted him to keep reading so he could find out what happened.

Danny, Del, and Doug prayed then. They asked God to be with Carmen and Maria Roper and give them a safe flight to Minneapolis, and they prayed for Clarence and Phil coming home. They even prayed for Eduardo, Mack, their mother, and the little ones. That embarrassed Eduardo for some reason, but it made him feel good too. He didn't know why, but he liked having them talk to God about him.

Shortly after they finished praying, Eduardo got up and went out. As he left the house he started for home, but halfway there he turned toward the pickup where he had hidden the pages of the Book his mother tore up. Maybe he'd be able to find that story about the Christian-killer and see how it ended.

He got the torn pages and began to scan them, using the dome light to read by. He couldn't find what he wanted to, but he did come across a lot of other stuff that was interesting, some of the things Jesus said about sin and going to heaven. Eduardo read those verses over and over again, hungrily, trying to make out what they said. He was so caught up in them that he didn't hear the Roper car drive up or the pickup door open.

"Eduardo!" Clarence Roper exclaimed, "What are you doing?"

He jerked upright, his face suddenly ashen.

"I didn't do it!" he cried defensively. "Honest, I didn't. I found it and decided to read it to–to see what–" His voice choked off.

"Don't get shook up about it. That's all right."

Clarence started to crawl into the cab beside the frightened boy but changed his mind and motioned Phil to do so.

For a moment the silence was a leaden barrier between them. Then Phil spoke quietly. "Do you understand what you're reading?"

Eduardo frowned. "Some of it."

"Maybe I can help you."

For a time Eduardo asked questions of the rancher's son, one after the other. He wanted to know how sin kept a guy from God and how Jesus Christ could give a person a new life. He couldn't understand it much better after Phil tried to explain it, but he began to see that he didn't have to understand all about it.

"God said that this was the way He is going to save us," Phil went on, "and that's all that really counts. If we confess our sin and put our trust in Jesus Christ, we can be saved."

Hope glimmered in Eduardo's eyes. "You mean that's all there is to it? It isn't any harder than that?"

"It's hard, all right," Phil acknowledged. "You've got to mean business with God and be willing to give Him full control of your life. But it's simple. And you can't earn it. Salvation is a free gift. All you have to do is accept it."

Eduardo thought about that. He didn't know why God was so good, but he knew that he wanted to become a Christian more than he wanted anything else in the world.

"Would you tell me how I can do that?" he wanted to know.

"Sure." Phil went over God's wonderful plan of salvation once more to make sure that Eduardo completely understood it. Then he told him how to pray, and they bowed their heads.

The eager boy had never really prayed before, but he told God that he was a sinner and that he was putting his trust in Jesus Christ to save him. When he finished, Phil prayed, asking God to give him understanding and courage to walk with Jesus Christ.

CHAPTER 11

THEN THERE WERE THREE

Eduardo wanted to go back to the house and tell Mack and his mother what had happened in his life, but he didn't quite dare. He could still remember how angry she had gotten at Mack when she found the Book in the saddlebag. What would she do if she learned that he, Eduardo, was a believer in this Jesus Christ? What would she say if she found out that he had turned his life over to Him?

He went to the house and straight to the bedroom he shared with Mack. He couldn't even tell his brother what had taken place in his life, although he was dying to do so.

Shortly after Danny Orlis took off to continue his trip to Mexico the next morning, Doug and Del went out with Phil to help build a fence. Mack was also with them, but Eduardo had to stay at home. He didn't go for that. He wished he could have been with the bigger guys. There were so many things that he wanted to ask them. But Mack had ordered him to stay at home, and Mamma had reinforced his order with her own.

"It's sure good to get back here again," Doug said.

"It's good to have you, isn't it, Mack?" Phil winked at his young friend. "Especially when we have to build fences and do a lot of other grubby jobs."

Mack grinned impishly. "Maybe we can get all the work done while they're here to help, Phil. Then we won't have anything to do for the rest of the summer except to go fishing and ride horseback."

"That'll be the day," Phil continued. "When we get one job finished, Dad will find a couple more for us to do."

"I suppose it's work for you guys," Del said, "but it seems like fun to Doug and me. We wouldn't mind if we had to do this sort of thing all the time, would we?"

Mack Flores shaded his eyes with his brown hand. The work they had to do was hard at times; but like Doug and Del, he found life on the Circle-R so interesting that even the hardest jobs were fun. And there was no greater boss in all the world than Mr. Roper. Mack hoped he could stay on the ranch and work when he grew up. There was nothing he would like better.

The only thing he didn't like about the Circle-R was the Sunday school the Ropers had started. He guessed it was all right, except that it bothered him so much that he couldn't sleep at night, and it had caused trouble between him and his mother for the first time since his father died.

When Sunday came, he decided that he wasn't going to the service in spite of the fact that the boys would be looking for him to be there. He just wouldn't go, and when he saw them later he'd think of something to tell them. He might have to lie to them a little, but that was better than lying to Mamma.

Sunday morning, when he came in to breakfast, his mother eyed him uneasily.

"You aren't going to Senor Roper's Sunday school today, are you, Mack?"

He shook his head indifferently. "Hadn't figured on it."

She was glad about that. Her smile chased the worry lines away, and she hummed a little tune as she fried tortillas for breakfast. Mack saw that Eduardo was uneasy, but he didn't know why and wasn't going to ask. He was still upset at his younger brother for letting Mamma know about the Book he had hidden.

As soon as Mack finished eating, he left the house and sauntered down to the barn. He could hide in there until Sunday school started. Then he would be safe.

But he didn't think Doug and Del would be in the barn helping feed the horses until one of them called out to him.

"I didn't know you were out here," Mack said, frowning his displeasure.

"We thought we'd better feed and water our horses before Sunday school."

"Oh." Coloring delicately, he turned and started to leave.

"You *are* going, aren't you?"

"Guess not. I've got things to do."

"We talked with your brother last night, and he said that he's coming."

"He *is?*"

"That's right," Del added. "Phil was telling me that his dad is going to ask Eduardo to say something this morning, so we know he's going to be there."

Mack had to go over that in his mind. There had to be some mistake. The ranch owner wouldn't ask Eduardo to say anything during Sunday school. This was probably Del and Doug's idea of a joke. Only that didn't sound like them.

"What's Eduardo going to talk about?" he asked curiously.

Doug's grin was tantalizing. "Why don't you come and find out?"

He nodded slightly. That was exactly what he was going to do, only he wasn't going alone. He'd see that Mamma was there to hear Eduardo too. He'd get even with that scheming brother of his. When Mamma got through with him, he'd be sorry he ever squealed about the Testament Mack had hidden in the barn.

It wasn't easy for Mack to get his mother to go to Sunday school that morning. She stormed about it when he first asked her and wanted to know why he had changed his mind.

"I can't tell you. Mamma," he retorted, "but I want you to come."

Her eyes narrowed. "Are you going to do something to shame me?" she asked.

"You know I wouldn't do that. I just heard that something's going to happen and I want you there to see it." He had gone as far as he dared. If she wouldn't come with that much urging, he would have to give up.

But he knew his mother well. She was still grumbling, but she put on her good dress and went over to Sunday school with him.

Eduardo's cheeks flushed as he saw his mother come in and sit down near the door. Mack smirked at him knowingly. Let him get up in front and talk now, when Mamma was there to hear.

He saw that his younger brother was squirming. The chances were that he would get up and scoot out of there before Mr. Roper had a chance to call on him. But that was all right too, because that would ruin Eduardo in the eyes of Phil and Del and Doug.

Eduardo did not get up and leave, however. He was trembling nervously, but he stayed there. And several minutes later when the rancher called on him, he stood and made his way to the front of the room. Clarence put an arm about his shoulder affectionately.

"Eduardo hasn't been to our Sunday school very much," he began, "but he's got something that he wants to share with us."

The boy cleared his throat and looked straight at his mother. "I–I didn't know that Mamma was going to be here this morning when I–I said that I'd get up and talk. Maybe I wouldn't have wanted to do it if I'd known she would be listening to me, but I'm glad you are here, Mamma. I've been wanting to tell you this ever since it–it happened but I haven't been able to."

Eduardo went on to tell about the Testament Mack had hidden in the barn. He told how he had given Mack's secret away and caused him to get slapped.

He even told how he got to wondering about the Book and what could be in it that would make his mother hate it so and how he had gathered up the pages and hidden them in the pickup.

"Then I sat in the ranch house the other night when Mr. Orlis and Del and Doug were having their Bible reading and prayer, and I decided to read that Book again. So I went out and was reading it when Mr. Roper and Phil came home. Phil showed me that I had to confess my sin and put my trust in Jesus Christ if I wanted to go to heaven. That's what I did."

He was staring directly at his ashen-faced mother.

"I became a Christian that night and I–I wanted to go right home and tell Mamma and Mack about it, but I was too scared. That's why I went to Mr. Roper and asked if I could tell what happened to me. I figured that way *everybody* would find out."

Mrs. Flores stood to her feet and started forward, her usually pleasant face a sallow mask.

"Come, Eduardo!" she exclaimed, grasping him firmly by the arm. "Come!"

Mack sat motionless while Mamma marched Eduardo out of the ranch house. He felt the muscles in his throat tighten. Eduardo would get cuffed on the side of the head or maybe beaten with a stick, but his older brother took no pleasure in it. Instead, he got to his feet.

"Mr. Roper?"

"Yes, Mack?" A hush was still over the little group.

"I have come to Sunday school many times and I–I've heard you talk about Jesus Christ. I want to follow Him, but I am afraid to. I am afraid because of Mamma and what she would think and say. Now my brother Eduardo has dared to confess his sin and walk with Jesus. I want to be a Christian too!"

Clarence Roper turned the meeting over to his son, Phil, and went into one of the bedrooms with Mack where they knelt and prayed.

"And now I want to go out and tell Mamma," the boy said.

"Do you want me to go with you?"

He shook his head. "I have to tell her what Jesus Christ has done for me."

The boy left the house as quickly as he could and hurried out to the house where his mother was sitting, anger and hurt mingling in her eyes.

"I am glad you got me to go to that Sunday school this morning," she said. "I would not have believed what I heard if I had not been there myself." Tears came to her eyes. "At least my oldest son still loves me and wants to do what I want him to."

The muscles in Mack's throat contracted. "I–I have to talk to you, Mamma."

"About what?"

"For a long time I've wanted to do what Eduardo did, but I've been afraid to do it because of what you would think and say. This morning he showed me that confessing my sin and letting Jesus Christ come into my life is the most important thing in all the world!"

She stared at him. "Mack! Not you, too!"

"I'm sorry, Mamma! I want to do what you want me to, but this Jesus Christ Mr. Roper talks about all the time *died* for *me* and *you* and the little ones. He died to save everyone!"

She started to cry. "I lose two sons."

"No, Mamma, you don't lose us. We will be better sons for you because we love Jesus."

She was hearing with her ears but not with her heart.

"Jesus did not stay dead," Mack went on. "He came back to life again and He's up in heaven fixing places for us to live so we can be with Him there.

All we have to do is to confess that we are sinners and that we believe Jesus and want Him to save us. And He will."

She turned that over in her mind. The people back in their village in Mexico were religious. And they talked about going to heaven when they died. But they had to work very hard in order to do it, keeping all the taboos and all the holy days. And even then they couldn't know for sure that the gods were going to have mercy on them and take them to heaven.

"You mean Senor Roper can tell me if I am going to heaven?" Such a hope was almost too great for her.

Mack had to think about that. "All I know is that when I confessed that I was a sinner and trusted Jesus to save me, Mr. Roper read me some verses that said I was going to heaven."

Mrs. Flores stood up and walked slowly over to the stove. There was a new interest stirring in her heart. She said nothing, but Mack read it in her face. He left the house and ran to get Clarence Roper. When they came back his mother was sitting in a rickety chair in the living room, a fat arm about Eduardo's slender waist.

"I brought Mr. Roper to talk to you, Mamma," Mack said.

"*Sí,*" she responded, nodding toward another chair.

He answered her questions and, before he left, was able to kneel and pray with her. Eduardo and

Mack knelt too, as happy as they had ever been in all their lives.

"Next, we talk to the little ones," their mother said when they finished praying. "I want them to know about this Jesus and that He died for them."

Doug and Del were in the living room with Phil when Clarence finally returned. They had been praying for him and for the boys and their mother. The three of them beamed when they learned that Mrs. Flores had also committed her life to Christ.

"I've never seen anything like it," Phil said. "I used to think that none of the Flores family would make decisions for Christ. Now there are three Christians in the family."

"Isn't it wonderful?" Doug exclaimed.

Del pulled in a deep breath. "And to think," he said quietly, "God used our devotions with Danny the first night we got here to touch Eduardo's heart and keep everything working."

"Yes, God used many things to answer our prayers for the Flores family," reflected Mr. Roper.

"It sure makes our coming down here worthwhile, doesn't it?"

There was no answer. There didn't have to be.

THE DANNY ORLIS SERIES

The Danny Orlis series, by Bernard Palmer, delivers a blend of adventure, mystery, and suspense through various settings—from the Canadian wilderness to Guatemalan jungles. Danny Orlis, an adept outdoorsman, skilled athlete, and committed Christian, employs his quick thinking, calm bravery, and biblical solutions to confront everyday problems and hair-raising dangers. Early stories focus on Danny navigating school life, sports, and outdoor challenges, while in later books, Danny and his wife Kay provide wisdom and guidance to youngsters facing lifelike situations and challenges. Having sold over two million copies, this series has made Palmer a renowned author in Christian youth literature. Palmer is also the author of the Felicia Cartright series and various other series for Christian youth.

AVAILABLE FROM WWW.ANEKOPRESS.COM